THE MAN WITHOUT

Ray Robinson was born in North Yorkshire in 1971. An award-winning short-story writer, his first novel, *Electricity*, is also published by Picador. He lives in London.

Also by Ray Robinson

Electricity

THE MAN WITHOUT

RAY ROBINSON

PICADOR

First published 2008 by Picador

an imprint of Pan Macmillan Ltd
Pan Macmillan, 20 New Wharf Road, London N1 9RR
Basingstoke and Oxford
Associated companies throughout the world
www.panmacmillan.com

ISBN 978-0-330-44071-4

9 8 7 6 5 4 3 2 1

A CIP catalogue record for this book is available from
the British Library.

Typeset by SetSytems Ltd, Saffron Walden, Essex
Printed and printed in the UK by
CPI Mackays, Chatham ME5 8TD

Visit **www.picador.com** to read more about all our books
and to buy them. You will also find features, author interviews and
news of any author events, and you can sign up for e-newsletters
so that you're always first to hear about our new releases.

for
VERONIQUE BAXTER
and
PETER WRIGHT

I

HE CLOSED THE staff office door behind him, took the letter out of his pocket and sat down to read, scooping mouthfuls of beans and sausage from his All Day Breakfast in a Can.

Dear Antony,
Following our assessment interview last Wednesday, I am writing briefly to give you my understanding of the outcome. You had previously been assessed by Dr Flagstaff in the Community Mental Health Team, who felt it appropriate for you to be assessed with a view to your psychological therapy . . .

Then he studied the questionnaire.

IMPORTANT – PLEASE READ FIRST

PLEASE READ EACH STATEMENT AND THINK HOW OFTEN YOU FELT THAT WAY OVER THE LAST WEEK.

1 I HAVE FELT TERRIBLY ALONE AND ISOLATED.
2 I HAVE FELT TENSE, NERVOUS OR ANXIOUS.
3 I HAVE FELT I HAVE SOMEONE TO TURN TO FOR SUPPORT WHEN NEEDED.
4 I HAVE FELT OK ABOUT MYSELF.

5 I HAVE FELT TOTALLY LACKING IN ENERGY AND ENTHUSIASM.

6 I HAVE BEEN PHYSICALLY VIOLENT WITH OTHERS.

7 I HAVE FELT ABLE TO COPE WHEN THINGS GO WRONG.

8 I HAVE BEEN TROUBLED BY ACHES, PAINS OR OTHER PHYSICAL PROBLEMS.

9 I HAVE THOUGHT OF HURTING MYSELF.

10 TALKING TO PEOPLE HAS FELT TOO MUCH.

11 TENSIONS AND ANXIETY HAVE PREVENTED ME DOING IMPORTANT THINGS.

12 I HAVE BEEN HAPPY WITH THE THINGS I HAVE DONE.

13 I HAVE BEEN DISTURBED BY UNWANTED THOUGHTS AND FEELINGS.

14 I HAVE FELT LIKE CRYING.

15 I HAVE FELT PANIC OR TERROR.

16 I MADE PLANS TO END MY LIFE.

17 I HAVE FELT OVERWHELMED BY PROBLEMS.

18 I HAVE HAD DIFFICULTY GETTING TO SLEEP OR STAYING ASLEEP.

19 I HAVE FELT WARMTH OR AFFECTION FOR SOMEONE.

20 MY PROBLEMS HAVE BEEN IMPOSSIBLE TO PUT TO ONE SIDE.

21 I HAVE BEEN ABLE TO DO MOST THINGS I NEEDED TO.

22 I HAVE THREATENED OR INTIMIDATED ANOTHER PERSON.

23 I HAVE FELT DESPAIRING OR HOPELESS.

24 I HAVE THOUGHT IT WOULD BE BETTER IF I WERE DEAD.

25 I HAVE FELT CRITICISED BY OTHER PEOPLE.

26 I HAVE THOUGHT I HAVE NO FRIENDS.

27 I HAVE FELT UNHAPPY.

28 UNWANTED IMAGES OR MEMORIES HAVE BEEN DISTRESSING ME.

29 I HAVE BEEN IRRITABLE WHEN WITH OTHER PEOPLE.

30 I HAVE THOUGHT I AM TO BLAME FOR MY PROBLEMS OR DIFFICULTIES.

31 I HAVE FELT OPTIMISTIC ABOUT MY FUTURE.

32 I HAVE ACHIEVED THE THINGS I WANTED TO.

33 I HAVE FELT SHAMED OR HUMILIATED BY OTHER
    PEOPLE.

34 I HAVE HURT MYSELF PHYSICALLY OR TAKEN
    DANGEROUS RISKS WITH MY HEALTH.

He was meant to tick one of the following boxes: NOT AT ALL (he noticed this usually scored zero points); ONLY OCCASIONALLY (usually one point); SOMETIMES (always two points); OFTEN (usually three points); MOST OR ALL OF THE TIME (usually a four).

THANK YOU FOR YOUR TIME IN COMPLETING THIS QUESTIONNAIRE.

— You're welcome.

It had been nearly three months since that day on the platform. His GP told him to wait at home for the Crisis Team and within the hour a man and woman appeared at his door. They sat in his room and listened as he told them about the train. They cleared their throats, scratched paper with pens, and said they'd put him down as URGENT.

But at least he had a date for his first appointment. A week today.

And a box of pills, unopened. Mirtazapine. 30 mg.

I HAVE FELT TERRIBLY ALONE AND ISOLATED.

Most or all of the time.

Four points.

There was a loud knocking at the staff-room door.

TALKING TO PEOPLE HAS FELT TOO MUCH FOR ME.

It was Derek. He stuck his overly large, bulbous head in, panting hard. You could never be sure where Derek was looking because his boss-eyes pointed east and west and always in opposite directions.

— Can. You. Spray. Cheese?

— Je ne say what?

— Say. Please?

— I'm on my break, Derek. Where are the other carers?

I HAVE BEEN IRRITABLE WHEN WITH OTHER PEOPLE.

Four points.

Derek got a palsied leg through the door, clanging his caliper against the jamb. A fist of wet, twisted fingers shook at Antony.

— Say (a huff and a puff) pleeeeease.

Derek staggered forwards. He'd made Antony a cup of tea and Antony was delighted to see Derek had spilt most of it down his trouser legs.

I HAVE FELT WARMTH OR AFFECTION FOR SOMEONE.

Then he heard Lerch out in the corridor, making abstract sounds, the motor of his electric chair clicking and whirring as he span in tight, rapid circles.

Antony took the tea from Derek. A peace offering.

— Thank you, Derek. That's *so* nice of you.

— You're. Welcome. Ant. Fanny.

Derek turned his face, clocking Antony with one beady, glassy eye, and Antony knew what he was thinking, because he was thinking it too: fucking wanker. But since Derek phoned Child Helpline the previous weekend the staff were no longer allowed to converse with him like adults.

The manageress had told Antony,

— You're on r-r-report. First v–verbal warning.

I MADE PLANS TO END MY LIFE.

As if.

She told the carers at yesterday's team meeting,

— No more banter with the the the c-clients.

She named no names but stared right at Antony.

I HAVE FELT HUMILIATED OR SHAMED BY OTHER PEOPLE.

F-f-four points.

Antony was sure that's why she got the job: pity. Because she was a stutterer, and obese to boot – because she *knew* what

6

it was like to be disabled by society. She wasn't employed on the basis of her managerial skill, that's for sure. And so now, because of Antony, they were all meant to treat Derek, this forty-year-old toss-bag, with kid gloves. Because he was *so* sensitive.

I HAVE THREATENED OR INTIMIDATED ANOTHER PERSON.

Antony looked at Derek's fat, puffy neck bulging over his shirt collar, and thought *ligature*, thought *airway obstruction*, thought *cerebral hypoxia* and *compression of the carotid artery*. Derek wiped the stringy saliva from his chin, sucked air through his lips, farted wearily, and staggered out.

THE DAY CENTRE offered a full range of development, training and leisure activities, from cookery to music to house-keeping and massage therapy, catering for the full range of physical disabilities: cerebral palsy, arthritis, spina bifida, multiple sclerosis, stroke, cystic fibrosis, amputees, deaf-blind, Hodgkin's disease, and so on. But Antony always got lumped with the more acutely disabled, and felt as if he'd been doing nothing but wipe arses for the past three years.

He eyed the clock: ten minutes before he returned to spoon-feeding, being puked on, chair-pushing, hoist-lifting, catheter-inserting, sticking useless shrivelled cock-ends into plastic receptacles. He took the bottle out of his locker: another sneaky-pete swig of Night Nurse to get him through the afternoon.

He closed his eyes, inhaling slowly, thinking about the night ahead. He pulled the top of his turtleneck down and stroked his throat, swallowing.

His skin *thrilled*. A smile tightened his face.

I HAVE HURT MYSELF PHYSICALLY OR TAKEN DANGEROUS RISKS WITH MY HEALTH.

You better make that another four.

HIS COLLEAGUES suggested an end-of-week drink in the Irish pub next to work. Antony made his excuses and got the bus home, which took forever and he just missed the end of *Neighbours*.

He watched the BBC news headlines. Three days since the planes went into the towers in New York. The TV said we are now at war with an invisible enemy and Antony thought *whatever* and switched it off.

He phoned his Auntie Val. The receiver purred and purred but no one picked up.

It was a worry.

He looked over at his bed. Recently, he'd taken to sleeping in it again. For months it had seemed like a snowy field, a bordered absence, uninviting, barren.

Some nights, he stared out of the window, glass in hand, thinking of ways to win Rebecca back. He imagined her figure lit by street lamps as she made her way towards the flat, but then he remembered watching her run along that very same street, three months before, and found himself cursing her.

He eyed the pencil and charcoal portraits of her tacked to the walls. He couldn't bring himself to take them down.

He poured himself a vodka and put some music on the stereo and stood before the window, watching Manchester growing dark outside.

It was a Friday night. He had only one thing to look forward to.

He'd run himself a bubble bath.

And begin.

WRAPPED in a silk kimono and twisting helix of smoke, he flicked through the new copy of *Harper's* until he found one: a model with a similar pair.

Same colour. Same misty, narrow look.

He took the scissors, cut carefully, and went over to the wall where the new face was beginning to emerge. He dabbed the back of the eyes with Pritt-Stick and positioned them above the nose from *Grazia*, the mouth from *Vogue*.

He tilted his head and squinted, exhaling sexy curlicues of bluish smoke.

HE BOUGHT a cheese-and-onion pasty from Greggs and decided to eat it in the park. He sat watching dog-walkers and children on bicycles, listening to some deafening bhangra coming from a lone sound stage. He remembered the previous summer, sunbathing with Rebecca over by the large chestnut tree near the bandstand, priming their tans before their holiday in Greece.

He dropped the half-eaten pasty in a bin and wandered into town, and though he knew he shouldn't, he strolled into Cheaper Sounds and went up to the cash desk and asked the manager in a sugary voice,

— Do you happen to have Rebecca's new contact details? I

have some things of hers that I know she'd *really* like me to return.

The manager looked at him wearily, sighed, and disappeared into the back room.

So Antony headed over the road to the Drapers' Arms and ordered a pint. He knew it was where the Cheaper Sounds staff usually went for a drink after work, but it got to 6:30 and no sign.

He wended his way down by the canal, to his dealer's squat.

IT WAS LATE by the time he got home. He rolled a J, poured some leftover wine, and booted up. The lime-green lights of the modem flickered. Already a stirring inside of him that he knew couldn't be staved. A few left-clicks took him to his Hotmail account. As per, his last message to Rebecca had returned:

```
    This is an automatically generated Delivery
Status Notification.
    Delivery to the following recipient failed
permanently:
```

He clicked the 'Rebecca' file and chose one from the top of the list.

The early days.

```
FROM: rebecca22@fishnet.com
SENT: 02 September 1998 19:45:22
TO: antmusic@hotmail.com
SUBJECT: Friday!
-----------------------------------------------
You're welcome darling – it's my pleasure. I'm
so excited about seeing you too! Every time we
are apart I miss you even more, and feel even
more excited at the prospect of seeing you
```

again. You're right, this really does get better and better all the time. I'm bursting with love for you and excitement about our future together.

　　love you xxxx

Thank you so much for doing this, and the whole Wales thing – I think you are so wonderful, I hope you know that. I am so excited about seeing you on Friday! And meeting me at the station – fantastic. This just gets better and better,
Speak soon,
Love you
A x x x

HE STARED HARD at the drawings of her body. DNA at its finest. Drawings on A1 newsprint, that's all he had left of her now. Charcoal, white chalk, finger-smudge. But he wanted to see her again. He wanted to smudge the *real* her. To know that she was happy. To make her happy. But he had no contact number. He couldn't ring her to give her a mouthful when he was drunk.

He walked over to the wall and pressed his face into the mirror. Through the shifting fog of his breath he saw two circular glints of iris slowly overlap like a Venn diagram, and then converge into one. He saw a molten drip hanging in a Latin-blue sky.

And then his reflection disappeared completely.

AN ABRUPT, searing spasm bent him double. Behind his eyelids he could still see that bright, molten sun, and then a song began whistling through his ears:

Everything But The Girl doing 'I Want Your Love'.

He got to his feet and saw the ghost of Rebecca sprawled across his unmade bed, the shapes of men moving across her body, like shadows. He heard their animal grunts; heard bodies slapping in a hot room.

Then a sibilant noise began to fill his ears.

He grabbed a lacy chemise off the floor and rammed it into his mouth. With his fingertip, he closed the jugular. With a bit more pressure, he reduced the blood flow through his carotid to a mere trickle. Maelstrom clouds, thick as migraines, began moving at high speed through his mind.

He controlled life, controlled death.

Beat.

The carotid, forked like a lizard's tongue. Above the arterial fork is the carotid sinus, cells sensitive to pressure and chemicals and once pressure is applied they can slow the heart right down . . .

To a beat.

He pressed, inhaled. Beat. Golden flowers bloomed behind his eyelids. Beat. He heard his panicked gasping. Beat. Saw high-speed clouds moving faster, faster. Beat. And then everything turned very cold.

No beat.

An icy turning.

No beat.

An iceberg rolling.

No beat.

No beat.

No beat.

And the woman in the mirror, she exhaled.

Hello?

His throat felt torn.

— Now then, son.

— Oh.

Jack. His father.

— I haven't woken you?

— No, Antony said.

— So how's tricks? Still seeing what's-her-face?

Antony walked over to the window and pulled the curtains. Light slapped him in the mush. Ahead, the red minaret of Strangeways' ventilation tower. Beyond that, the faceless grey slabs of City and Portland Towers.

— Hello?

— Yeah, Antony said. Hunky dory.

— Good, good. Just don't be making me a grandfather yet.

Antony searched for his tobacco as Jack jabbered on. He could hear his half-brother shouting something in Catalan in the background. He found a docked rollie in the ashtray and lit the end.

But he missed the sudden shift in his father's voice.

— I'll be flying into Teesside tonight, Jack said.

— What?

— Back to England.

— What for?

Jack sighed.

— Someone left a copy of the *Northern Echo* in the bar yesterday. I saw the obituary and rang home. To check like.

— Who?

— Val, Jack said. Your Auntie Val.

Antony fell inside.

— Do you want me to call you back?

— Val?

— Haven't you?

— No.

— Funeral's tomorrow afternoon, Jack said. Thought I'd show my respect. Besides, I've a bit of unfinished business. You're coming, right?

Antony thumbed the red icon to hang up.

HE TOOK the two photographs out of their frames, cracked and dog-eared from years of travelling around in his back pocket. No matter how he's felt, how angry or disappointed he's been, they've always been with him, his 2D chaperones.

Jack, sat at the end of a table with Val on her eighteenth-birthday night. His laugh-a-lot grin and bushy, crow-black hair. And the photograph of his mother showed a young woman twisting her body and bending a knee. Dark roots in her bleached hair that seemed so incongruous, so unlikely.

Antony tried crossing his eyes to see the blur of him.

But he couldn't.

He asked Jack once,

— How come you two got together in the first place?

But Jack just fed him the same old shite that she did, and Antony just couldn't figure it out.

Jack in Spain with his new family. Mother at home with Lou.

HE WAS TEN YEARS OLD when Val gave him the photograph. He remembered going round to hers and finding Eddie there, drinking. Eddie was no relation, just an old bloke from the village, but over the years he'd become something of a surrogate father to Antony. The two adults shared looks and Eddie went,

15

— Show him.

Antony brought the photograph close to his face. He made out Val straight away; her beehive looked bigger than ever. She was sitting with a group of people around a long table.

— It were taken at the Social on me eighteenth, she said. Fancied the arse off the singer. Did the Stones to a tee.

She raised her eyebrows at Eddie.

— Should've married him instead of that useless Irish cunt. Here, that's him.

A long red fingernail next to a young bloke: dark hair, large sideburns.

— Your singer? Antony said.

Her crooked smile.

— Your dad, Antony. Your frigging dad.

His father's absence.

— Jack, Val said quietly. His name's Jack Ellis. A cockney. Up here to do some building work and stayed on.

Eddie's pale, apple-green eyes.

— You want to meet him.

It wasn't a question.

Antony looked down at his shoes and shrugged.

— Thought as much.

AND HEARING Jack's voice on the phone that morning, Antony felt that childish anticipation, that longing to hear his father say it,

— I'm sorry, son. For leaving you with them.

ALL DAY he avoided reminiscing, filling his mind with empty tasks. But as he undressed and climbed into bed and lay poised on the edge between wakefulness and sleep, he saw the cartoonish blur of Val's face and her deep platform shoes – her Magic Joe Cocker Boots, she called them. He saw the Regal King Size hanging from the side of her heavily lipsticked gob, and the whole affair was surmounted, as usual, by her huge silvery beehive.

He necked the Mirtazapine and within five minutes he was already starting to feel twatted. He did a quick Net search on the drug, to get the low down, but it appeared it was safe. No history of mass lemming-style suicides.

Mirtazapine. Formula: $C_{17}H_{19}N_3$. Elimination half-life: 20–40 hours.

Side effects occurring commonly:

increased appetite
weight gain
drowsiness
dizziness
headaches
general or local swelling.

Side effects occurring rarely:

mania
nightmares
vivid dreams
seizures
tremor
muscle twitching
pins and needles
rash and skin eruptions
pain in the joints or muscles
low blood pressure.

Surfing left him with e-nausea and he had to lie down, and when he closed his eyes his inner world was pixellated – he found it strangely reassuring.

But then it hit him. Shit: tomorrow. His Monday outreach session with Kenneth.

He staggered over to the phone, the sedative-effect of the M dragging him under. He pressed the number for the Centre and let it purr.

There's no one here to take your call at the moment, but if . . .

He cleared his throat.

— Hi, Antony, it's Trudy. I'm afraid I won't be in today. There's been a death in the family and, well, it's important I go to the funeral, you know. Anyway, I've sorted Kenneth's cover, so don't . . .

He hung up.

Antony, it's Trudy.

— Fuck!

He collapsed onto the bed, burying his face into Rebecca's T-shirt.

HE HADN'T SLEPT so well in years – a powerful, Snow-White sleep – but he knew he couldn't afford to be smacked-up today.

Home.

Today was the day, and it was bigger than anything he'd ever known before.

He stepped to it. He ironed his best shirt and trousers and at 7:30 he phoned the Care Support Team. He knew the day shift would be in their office by then, sat in their poky kitchenette, gossiping over coffee and digestives.

Someone picked up with a sleepy sigh.

He told the woman it had to be 8:30 or nothing.

— This is *very* short notice, she said.

— But that's your job. That's why we pay you.

He heard her wilting.

— And it has to be half-eight, you say?

— No later. Kenneth's wife has to be at work. You can't leave him more than five minutes, max. He'll go walkabout. You know this.

— I'll see what I can do.

— No. You'll phone Chris. He can be there in ten minutes, if he can get his fat arse out of bed, that is.

I HAVE FELT TOTALLY LACKING IN ENERGY AND ENTHUSIASM.

Antony hung up.

He hated having to do this to Kenneth, dumping those useless fuckers on him. Kenneth needed routine, familiarity; he needed someone to prompt, to reassure, and to operate his aides-memoires. Not those bone-idle arse-wipers.

— I'm sorry, Kenneth.

He went into the bedroom and looked at his bag.

He couldn't believe he was doing this.

THE TRAIN was there on the platform, waiting, doors opened wide. Three hours on the Transpennine Express, that's all it took to get back there.

Home. How it had pulled him into fragments.

The train was like a threat, waiting to materialize.

He remembered being at this very station three months before. How the train had swept his hair sideways and sucked the breath from his mouth. The woman's outline reflected in the flicker of the carriage windows.

He dropped his bag.

I HAVE A TERRIFYING CONVICTION SOMETHING BAD IS GOING TO HAPPEN.

Racing heartbeat.

Dry mouth.

Chest pain.

Rapid breathing.

Palpitations.

And the thought of all of the above – that just created more anxiety. It expressed itself through intense muscle pain and sickening dizziness. He was distorting. He was feeding back. Symptoms causing anxiety causing panic causing fear causing symptoms causing . . .

Like he was trapped in the echoing Tannoys.

He inhaled, gulped.

Fuck.

I HAVE FELT PANIC OR TERROR.

He could see a train coming in on the opposite platform.

He stepped back. He ran.

Heard himself panting, laughing.

Up the stairs, over the footbridge, down the other side.

He had no idea what he was doing.

A train on the platform.

He didn't know.

Doors opened.

Hadn't a clue.

But the weight had lifted.

The weight had gone.

He jumped on.

HE FOUND HIMSELF IN a small town he'd never heard of before. The sign on the platform said *Welcome to Todmorden* and some funny-bugger had written beneath: *You'll never leave.* Hills filled the skyline in every direction and the town snaked along the bottom of a deep, narrow valley, gashed by the tarred windpipe of a canal. Terraced houses clung to the sides of jutting crags and fresh moor-air misted across his face, reminding him of something he'd rather not be reminded of.

The first stab of guilt: I'm letting Val down.

At the bottom of the hill he spotted the Fox and Goose.

The pissing rain was getting heavier. He tied his hair back with a laggy band.

THE CAREWORN FACES of flat-capped old men followed him as he walked between the tables and smoke. He ordered a bitter and found a seat beside two bulky, ugly bastard men, hoeing crisps into their gobs like a pair of stevedores, their Northern accents so thick it surprised him.

He noticed a fella chatting up some young woman at the other end of the bar. He wore a cheap blue suit and had bad hair and looked like a complete Norbert. The sort with blisters on his thumbs from playing video games. His face: smile stretching from ear to ear, eyes slitted; but hers said resignation, like she'd rather be anywhere. Norbert caught Antony staring and turned a cold shoulder. Antony coughed for no reason, rolled a rollie and sucked a few inches off his pint, watching how her smile missed her long-distance eyes.

He liked her, but didn't know why.

He could sense indiscreet piercings, wasted summers at muddy festivals, baggy jumpers and paint-splattered dungarees. The type, actually, that did his head in at art school. Earth Mothers with an unhealthy obsession for nebulous shite like Fate and astrology and crystals and auras and chakras and holistic fucking healing.

But he pictured a tattoo on the base of her spine: butterfly wings, spread.

She slapped Norbert's arm.

— Fuck off, will you!

And Jesus, he was getting up. He was walking over there. Cells of violence transubed within him, body surging with adrenalin, the buzz, the Power of Man in his bones. But he couldn't feel his legs.

In a tone unmistakable for aggression he said,

— Did you hear the lady?

Norbert stepped back, body sideways on.

The girl eyed Antony up and down.

— What the fuck, she said, has it got to do with you?

— Sorry. I just thought.

— Aye, well, you know what 'thought' did.

He laughed; it's something Val used to say.

— Thought I'd shat myself, but it was just a wet fart?

Her laughter made heads turn.

Antony's spine tingled. His eyes were drawn to the gap in her top: hint of ample, soft, utter kissableness. He coughed, shrugged, and shuffled back over to his seat.

Behind him: the loamy stench of geraniums dotted along the windowsill, bringing him back down to earth.

HE CHECKED his mobile.

— Where are you?

It was Kenneth.

— Why aren't you here?

Then a voice in the background and the dead tone.

Antony wasn't there that morning, so Kenneth had gotten his number, hunted it out, and dialled. Which meant that he'd been able to access what?

His procedural memory?

His temporal-coding facility?

By two o'clock he'd had a bowl of chips and three packets of prawn-cocktail crisps and the Bastard Thirst had started kicking in. That three-pint-point of no return. It looked like she was onto her sixth.

As soon as Norbert skedaddled, with a valedictory glare, she came and plonked herself down next to Antony. It turned out Norbert was an ex, trying to get back in her good books. Antony went, Lunchtime booty call, and she laughed that laugh.

She told him how she'd been unemployed for two years after finishing her A-levels (euphemistically 'having time out' despite three A grades), had lived in Todmorden all her life, and no of course she was too young to be married, and no she didn't have any kids, but yes she liked her lager and lime and Marlboro Lights and midday Monday drinking sessions at the Fox and Goose, thank you very much.

She was staring at him again. Telltale remnants of mascara?
— So what do you do? No, don't tell me: bank manager.
— Funny. I'm a care worker.
The second real stab of guilt: I'm letting Kenneth down.
You know, she breathed. But she didn't finish.
She stood up and straightened her skirt.
— My brother used to have a carer when he was young.
— What's his disability?

She raised an eyebrow.

— He's deaf, but he's a fucking dude. He's a deejay, does deaf raves, and he fucking hates being called disabled.

He noticed then, how she spoke with her hands.

— Care for another, Mr Carer?

He wanted to fingerspell a response, but just nodded.

THREE DRINKS LATER their knees were touching and she was saying,

— I like to get back into bed and eat muesli while listening to audio books from the library. Don't laugh. I'm on Ted Hughes at the moment. *Crow*. Fuck he's got a sexy voice. Shame he carked it. He grew up round here.

— And Henry Moore.

— Henry Moore what?

— The landscape round here, inspired him.

— And the Brontës. They grew up the other side of the moor. So?

Antony shrugged and asked her what she liked doing at the weekend.

— Er, getting *wasted*. Oh, and I love the fact that, you know, I can lie in bed till two in the afternoon and not feel guilty about it. You?

— The gym, the movies, nice walks in the country.

She squeezed his upper arm; he flexed.

— You've never seen the inside of a gym, mister.

Her touch sent neurons firing.

His hypothalamus literally *ejaculated* endorphins.

But she pulled her arm back and cleared her throat softly, fist to mouth.

— Really, though?

She felt it.

— Same as every twenty-six-year-old, he said. I'm either in the process of getting drunk or recovering from the process of getting drunk.

They chinged their glasses together and he realized that not only was he six years older than her but that he was holding in his stomach and puffing out his chest like some sad middle-aged twat.

Then she said, apropos of fuck-all,

— Have you ever seen a dead person?

Breath rushing out of his mouth, but he felt nothing.

— Sorry, she said.

— It's OK.

The X of her eyes focused sharply and her lovely mouth went,

— I didn't mean.

— It's just. Just I'm meant to be at a funeral today.

He looked at his watch, the numerals of its iris.

— Should be over by now.

She leaned back, extended a hand.

— I'm sorry. I don't even know your name.

And something gave. Something definitely shifted.

He wanted to touch her.

He needed to touch her.

HE LAUGHED light-heartedly as they walked across the road
to the pizza place. That bald directness – he got the
impression here was a young woman who usually got her own
way. And why not, when you looked like that?

— So you coming home with me or what then?

She told him she lived 'up on the tops' and that her
flatmate wouldn't be back from work 'while six'.

He pictured a dank cottage with ethnic hangings and soot-
blown walls.

— Party needn't end here, Mr Antony.

TENSION AND ANXIETY HAVE PREVENTED ME FROM
DOING CERTAIN THINGS.

— Sorry. I'd love to. But I can't.

She fell into a silent pout and flipped her cigarette away.
He gave her his mobile number and said it'd be great to see
her again. She raised her perfect eyebrows and started flirting
with the Asian guys behind the counter.

— Can I get a home delivery again? Please. My feet are
proper killing me.

One of them ducked through the hatch and brought her
pizza box through. She followed the guy out the door; Antony
followed her to the pizza van.

— You sure you don't want to come up?

He looked at his watch, shrugged.

— I've really got to get back.

She climbed into the back of the van, sat on some boxes and went,

— Proper home delivery.

She pulled the van door shut and was gone.

ON THE TRAIN back to Manchester, he closed his eyes and imagined what could've been happening. He saw Jade's drowsy, long-lashed smokiness. Saw her full lips parting in a post-come narcosis. Saw himself snorting coke from between her breasts. Imagining the jealousy he'd feel when he touched her body. He was sure he'd never see her again.

HE POPPED HIS M, took off his shoes and lay on the bed.

Home. Going back there tomorrow? Those streets. Those houses. That churchyard. Val, dead.

He remembered blonde sticks of splintered kindling and the heady smell of Duraglit, fire banked high, cracking and spitting, and how the tangerine-flicker dancing across her living room would hypnotize him.

Val was a mucky cow, always clarted up to the eyeballs and looking ridiculous in her miniskirts and beehive hairdo. She had a mouth on her as well; pimento-tongued. But he often wished he could live with her instead of Mam and Lou. OK, her house was disgusting; it was probably the scummiest house on the estate; it stank of cat piss and the wallpaper was coming off the walls and the carpets were threadbare and stained.

But at least she did it with men.

He'd hear her alarm go off upstairs and put the fire guard round and go into the kitchen and bring the kettle back to the boil and carry the sweet milky tea up to her.

She would look at him narrowly, blinking in the lamplight.

She'd made an empty house. Their things lying around: Mikey and Barry and Lily's clothes. Photographs of the three of them in summer.

He tried to remember his cousins as kids, but all he could remember was trouble.

Lying on Val's bed, chin in hands, he'd watch her transform herself from a lined, fatigue-faced woman, into a caricature of self-belief.

He knew he couldn't do it, that train journey back there tomorrow.

He stared at the ceiling, willing his heart to decelerate.

— I'm sorry, Val.

HE ARRIVED AT THE usual time of 8:30 a.m., knocked and walked in. Lizzie, standing beside the kitchen table, coat buttoned and handbag poised, gave him a weary look and left without uttering a word.

Kenneth was sat at his computer playing *Shit Scrabble Fuck*. He eyed Antony curiously and went,

— Why do you do this?

— Do what, Kenneth?

— This do-gooding?

Antony hung his coat on the back of a chair and shrugged.

— Guess I must've done something bad in a previous life?

— Or this life, Antony. Or this one.

Kenneth had spent many years leading a successful life as a Unitarian priest.

Then the disease, then the brain damage, then the amnesia.

The triptych of Kenneth's pathology.

Physically he was fine – apart from a slight stagger and a tendency to walk too fast – it was just his memory stopped at seventeen years old. Inside his head, it was still 1967. Harold Wilson was Prime Minister and 'All You Need is Love' was at number one.

Antony stared at the back of Kenneth's head, wondering what he must think when he looked in the mirror and saw a greying, myopic man squinting back, and not a freckle-faced youth. It's lucky Kenneth and Lizzie were childhood sweet-hearts and he recognized her; Kenneth often told Antony how he fell in love with her every day, all over again. How he listened for her footsteps. How he sniffed the air for her perfume.

After a quick game of *Shit Scrabble Fuck* – where expletives scored the highest and which Kenneth always won – they had their first of many Coffee and Fag Breaks. Kenneth didn't smoke until he lost his memory, but as soon as he came out of the coma and his aphasia had departed he was asking for Marlboros! Marlboros! Marlboros! Smoking became his favourite pastime – so much so that Lizzie demanded he set strict Fag Breaks for himself, otherwise he'd happily sit and chain-smoke himself to death.

Cigarettes, more than anything else, gave Kenneth's life structure, meaning.

On the wall, next to the kettle, Antony had pinned some picture-mnemonics of Kenneth's care team; Antony's was a red ant with the word 'Dob' and a picture of a baby wearing blue. Next to that: Coffee, milk, one sugar.

— So what's my name? Antony said.

Kenneth turned his back to the wall and clicked his fingers.

— Your name is Antony cunting Dobson. My bastard conscience.

And to think he was once a Man of God!

— So what now?

Kenneth gawped around the room.

— What, you fucker?

— What do we need to do now?

Antony watched him squint at the labels on the cupboards:

CUTLERY
TEA + COFFEE
PLATES + BOWLS
POTS + PANS

Then the labels on the doors:

CLOAKROOM
TOILET
LIVING ROOM
STAIRS

Antony cleared his throat, nodding towards the wall planner. Kenneth tutted and staggered over there, drawing a finger across the columns and eyeing the clock a few times before going into the cloakroom.

ANTONY TOOK his arm as they climbed the mossy steps out of the house.

— So which way?

Kenneth had lived on this street for decades, but still he looked up and down, a painful caricature of incomprehension. Then something triggered a response; he pulled the prompt cards from his pocket: images, arrows, scribbled words. Further aides-memoires. Coping strategies.

Walking to the post office, to pick up Kenneth's DLA cheque, was always a treacherous affair. The formal risk assessment Antony had to produce for the short journey was twelve pages long. At the post office, Antony waited for Kenneth to sort out where he was and for what reason.

— Post office. Stamps. No. Envelopes. Cunt. Post office. No.

Then Kenneth was into the swing of things, repeating the same lewd dialogue with the counter girl, as if it was rehearsed, as if they shared the joke.

When they eventually got back they had another Coffee and Fag Break and then they played some music. Kenneth, the ex-Servant of Christ, loved The Who, and he was a mean piano player – a fact that didn't come to light until after his illness.

Antony accompanied Kenneth on an old acoustic guitar and they played 'Pinball Wizard' and then 'My Generation' until he noticed sweat-rings under Kenneth's arms.

Upstairs, a door was slammed.

Sarah, a cute but taciturn eighteen-year-old, made her scruffy descent. She entered the room, clearly hung-over and unamused by the din, muttering a hello. She went into the kitchen and slammed a few cupboard doors.

Kenneth, his nose touching the sheet music, sang,

— Who Are You? ooh-ooh, ooh-ooh.

Kenneth used to be violent towards her, this odd invader who looked like a relative, but, he was convinced, wasn't. They'd had to ask her not to call him Dad, just Kenneth. She didn't seem to mind.

Sarah headed back up the stairs without looking at either of them.

Antony checked his watch; bang on cue there was a rap at the door. Another of Kenneth's sizeable care team.

— Right. I'm off now, mate.

Kenneth's eyes narrowed as he said,

— When we going for that pint?

— Maybe next week. Have a good weekend, yeah.

Chris bumbled into the room.

— All right, Rev?

He plonked himself down on the settee and started searching for the remote.

Kenneth glared at the fat intruder.

WATCHING GIRLFRIENDS, following them into the bathroom. Women's magazines and years of bad mistakes. His expertise with the palette from his years at art school. Hue, texture, shade. The Science of Colour Theory. The art block was situated next to the training parlours for hairdressers and beauticians. Days with his face pressed against the glass, watching immaculate young women dress and cut rows of severed heads.

HE SAT THERE watching the ten o'clock news on the telly, wondering why they'd stopped showing the scenes of the planes going in, the towers coming down.

He closed his eyes and saw Jade lying naked beside him, tired eyes blinking at him through sleep-jumbled hair, inflecting a croaky, sexy good morning . . .

The sound of his mobile rousted him from the reverie.

— Where were you?

Antony walked over to his window. Manchester was lit up outside, its cool blue and white neon so vivid against the roily Northern sky.

He heard the noise of echoing Tannoys.

— Hello?

— I'm here.

— I thought, Jack said. Thought you'd've come.

— I couldn't get the time off work.

— I'm at the airport.

Antony pictured Jack amid the human bustle.

— Your Barry was there. Said the three of them are splitting the house.

— Was our Lily there? Mikey?

— Just your Barry.

— Was *she* at the funeral?

— Your mum?

37

— A-huh.

— She moved to Cornwall months ago. I thought . . . ?

— No.

Jack said she'd been ill with the drink, and that Lou had gone.

Antony heard himself say it,

— She can rot.

But inside he felt the pounding weight of total, utter abandonment.

— Isn't it about time, Jack said, that you two made amends?

— The fact you even said that.

— I'm sure she still loves you, you know.

Antony hung up.

HE'D SPENT most of his life working out the relationship they never had. He used to make up an entirely different biography for himself, where Jack broke out of prison when Antony was a baby, jumped from the high prison wall into a tree, breaking an arm, a collarbone, just so Jack could come home to watch him sleeping, and he'd stand beside Antony's cot, tears streaming down his face as he realized: absence is far stronger than presence. He'd hand himself in, broken, regretful.

Meeting Jack only made it worse; Antony could see himself in him.

— Well, Jack had said, there's no need for a DNA test, is there?

Antony hated the fact that he looked like him, moved like him; same gestures, same hands, same gait. His double helices stained more with the Y of Father than the X of Mother. Inescapable. Ineluctable.

Whenever Antony thought of Jack, he remembered the first time they met, laced with the smell of the prison. Of piss. Spunk.

The frontal cortex is the MONITOR. The Hippocampus is the HARD DRIVE. The perceptual cortices are the DESK-TOP GUIs.

Is K's amnesia a deficit of encoding, storage or retrieval? Twenty-seven years of memories, of experience, gone. No trace. The virus has cyberattacked his hard drive.

The amber of memory: the glue that binds.

THE MANAGERESS was vexed.

— You want two hour-hours off ev-ev-ev-ev-every F-Friday?

— I'll go straight from Kenneth's. I'll get my lunch on the way and I'll be back here no later than three, to help with the afternoon rush.

— This is highly ir-ir-ir (the painful wait for the stutterer to finish, the biting of lips, commanding the face to remain inert, not to shout: FUCKING SPIT IT OUT!) ir-reg-reg-reg (and the unsupportive memory of Kenneth doing his Roger Daltrey impression: *Why don't you all, f-f-f-f-fade away*) reg-regular.

— I have a letter from the doctor. I know, I should've said something sooner . . .

She span in her chair, lifting a hand to signal he should leave.

Fuck her.

THURSDAY AFTERNOONS meant Smoke Club. The group convened in the smokers' Portakabin to play chequers and cards, to drink tea and gripe. Smoke Club currently consisted of eight clients, their ages ranging from thirty to sixty-five, all of whom chain-smoked, hence the name. On the back of the cabin door, one of them had stuck a poster:

> The **first** rule about **Smoke Club** is
> you don't talk about strokes, or
> blood clots, or ischemia, or
> cholesterol, or embolisms, or
> thrombosis, or CONSULTANTS!!!
>
> The **second** rule about **Smoke Club**
> is you don't talk about VICTIMS!!!

They all sat in their usual circle, all perky and totally Game On! Puffing away, hoisting floppy arms and legs around like dead relatives.

A new member joined last week. The stroke had hit him particularly hard and the only word he could manage to utter was,

— Tea tea tea tea tea tea.

Foolishly, Antony asked again,

— Would you like a cup of tea?

The man looked at him askance.

— Tea! Tea tea tea tea tea!

A few of the left-hemiplegics had experienced anomia, the word-finding difficulty, and Antony had seen how it led not only to insurmountable frustration but, in most cases, a complete loss of self.

The painful *err* of failed lexical retrieval.

The flickering screen of the fucked-up word-processor.

The total blackout of the crashed semantic system.

The paused, wide-eyed, tip-of-the-tongue states.

And their failings always left them shame-faced, afraid to make eye contact in case they looked at you and forgot the word *human*.

The new guy was getting irate,

— TEA! TEA! TEA! TEA! TEA!

AT ONE POINT during that afternoon, Antony discovered one of the Smokers used to know Kenneth; she said they'd accessed the same services a few years ago, shortly after Kenneth's amnesia struck.

— He acted like a complete psycho, she said. Everyone feared him.

Antony nodded.

WHEN HE GOT HOME, he opened the file on his laptop again: What's the Frequency, Kenneth? Mainly notes from the many books he'd been reading on memory loss, trying to gain some insight, to better understand.

K's aetiology. Initial presentation, November 1995: flu-like symptoms, fatigue, severe headaches, followed rapidly by coma, lasting 26 days. In the acute stage following the coma, K was aphasic — unable to understand spoken or written language — and hemiparetic. FES-based gait therapy with a physiotherapist proved successful.

The virus caused bilateral lesions in the anterolateral and medial portions of the temporal lobes, insula and putamen. Non-verbal and visual memory — memory for faces and names, autobiographical memory, and certain spatial aspects of stimuli — has been severely affected due to damage to the right temporal regions.

Owing to the preservation of the frontal lobe regions, K
has some insight into his memory loss.
How much is *some?*

He didn't know how Kenneth coped. When he was with
Kenneth, Antony wondered what movement or thought must
be like without memory; without it, we have no story, and
without a story we're nothing.

But there were times Antony didn't want to remember.
There were times he thought Kenneth was lucky.

SUN MOTES DAPPLED his eyelids. His mind was somersaulting. He climbed out of bed and moaned as the room span. His head always pounded for days afterwards, the whites of his eyes pinked with blood, the angry constriction in his throat.

He turned the gas fire on full whack and forced a glass of milk down his throat.

On the bathroom mirror, he found the words I LOVE YOU written in lipstick.

And the stab of it: his reflection. His spectral doppelgänger. The daydream him. Sleepwalk him. Mascara-and-lippy-smudge him.

He tried to smile, but it was more of a grimace.

He stood in the shower for ages.

Removing her from his body.

TOMORROW WAS his first meeting with the psych. He imagined the man or woman peering at him over half-moon glasses, a look of contempt feeding their face, deadpan as a Magritte figure. He couldn't help it: he started preparing arguments.

LIZZIE OPENED the door. She put a hand on his chest and stepped out.

She began to sob.

— I don't know, she said, how long I can put up with this for.

Antony folded his arms.

— Do you know Kenneth phoned me on Monday?

She started to laugh. There was a meanness in her eyes and an unwelcome statistic popped into Antony's head: two thirds of women whose male partner acquires a disability leave them within a year. But he quickly reminded himself that he had no idea what it was like to live with Kenneth, and that he had no right to judge.

— I can only guess, Lizzie. But you've got to admit, he's making progress.

She sighed.

— But he's . . .

A sober pause.

— He's what?

Nothing.

— You can tell me.

She lifted the sleeve of her coat: her forearm, smeared with bruises.

Antony watched her walk away.

THEY WERE MAKING their way back from the post office when Kenneth came to a halt outside the Black Sheep.

Antony had been dreading this moment.

— How about that pint, cunt features?

Antony made the mistake of hesitating; Kenneth stumbled in. The barmaid eyed them both.

— Your medication, Kenneth. I'm not sure it's a . . .

— My bastard conscience, are we?

Antony sighed.

— A fucking child, am I? Fucking idiot?

— No. You're not.

Kenneth took out a cigarette and lit it with a flourish.

— Two pints of your finest ale, sweet cheeks.

Although not strictly a sackable offence, Antony realized this was perhaps not the wisest of career moves, but he was sure Kenneth would get halfway through his first mouthful and be bored rigid, and the homing instinct would kick in.

But no: Kenneth sat and chain-smoked, ignoring Antony's appeals, sucking the pint down in a few thirsty gobfuls.

His eyes, Antony noticed, had an unusual sparkle to them.

Antony checked his watch.

— Better make a move now, Kenneth.

— Make mine another pint.

— But we need to hand over to Chris.

Antony stood up and put his jacket on.

— Sweet cheeks, another of your finest ales and make it *snappy*.

— Kenneth, please.

— Sit down, fuck face.

Antony got an inkling of the true velocity of Kenneth's temper. He sat down as Kenneth's pint arrived. Kenneth took a heavy mouthful, sighed, and leaned back.

Antony had never seen him looking so content, but he seemed to have forgotten what he was saying. This, at least, was normal.

Antony phoned the house and Sarah answered.

— When Chris arrives . . .

— He's here.

— Tell him to come down to the Black Sheep immediately.

He watched Kenneth trying to make a sensory analysis of the information.

Cognition failure. Storage capacity: nowt.

He grabbed Antony's arm.

— The white-coat cunts, they wouldn't let me in to see her, you know.

— See who?

Antony was thinking it was just another one of Kenneth's semantic word games: Antony takes the lead and Kenneth follows in a phonological loop and they pretend that Kenneth's memory is anything *other* than temporally immediate.

— Go on.

Kenneth took out another cigarette and lit it with the one in his mouth.

A few minutes of muscular silence passed between them until Chris appeared in the doorway, throwing Antony a You're-In-The-Shit-Now look.

— Kenneth?

— That's my name, don't wear it out.

— Who wouldn't they let you in to see?

Kenneth glared at Chris.

— Where's the toilet, fat fuck? Take me.

And with that, they were gone.

So there he was. The day, the hour, the moment. Sat in the Community Mental Health Team waiting room, totally out there with uncertainty. The idea of playing his script on someone else's stage, to the cold eyes of psychotherapy.

But suddenly it felt like his whole life had been leading up to this moment: in this waiting room about to meet a complete stranger who'd help him piece together the fragments. To finally be at home with himself. But the fear of giving it a voice. The sudden apprehension of revealing something so private.

He was relieved to see that the psych was a man.

They both extended a hand, and suddenly he didn't want to do this, to be like this, to have this drive.

He followed the man along the corridor, fingering the questionnaire in his pocket.

ON THE BUS back to the Centre, he listened to Jade's message for the third time. She apologized for being drunk and lairy on Monday, and then,

— Why don't we meet up this weekend in Manchester? My brother's deejaying at a deaf rave in Fallowfields. If you fancy coming, let me know, we can meet for a drink beforehand. But bring some earplugs, it gets proper loud.

His guts turned liquidy. His face tightened with an idiotic smile.

And so he listened to her voice for the fourth time.

It helped erase the memory of what had just happened.

THAT NIGHT'S SOUNDTRACK was Daft Punk's *Homework*. He stuck the plug in and ran a bubble bath, and then rolled a fatty J and poured a tall vodka.

He scanned his collection: lacy black and white knickers and bras, slips, skirts, tights, heels, girdles, chokers, stockings, suspenders, silky nightgowns, blouses, garter belts. He selected an outfit and spread it across his bed. Then he went into the bathroom and lowered himself into the hot bath. He closed his eyes, trying to relax, but the excitement of the night ahead was making him churn. He placed a hot flannel over his neck and face for a few minutes, and then shaved again, precisely, against the grain.

Not thinking about the psych. Not thinking about that room. The words that were said in there.

He climbed out of the bath, dried and moisturized, and then pulled tonight's dress on.

He applied the Blue Jaw cover, eyeliner, a high-coverage matte cream to powder foundation, and then the lippy: a pencil line along the vermilion border, shaping the philtrum with a V.

Then the eyeshadow, a single-pallet powder and brush, and finally the mascara.

And then he tucked. He lay on his back with his legs in the air and pulled his scrotum tight. His balls moved up towards the base of his shaft, and with a little jiggle they slid into the cavity in his groin.

He pulled his tights up, and the feeling, the look of them?

I HAVE BEEN HAPPY WITH THE THINGS I HAVE DONE.

He began to strut around the room, feeling a need to touch everything, to sidestep and sashay, end-of-catwalk pirouette. He *thrilled* at the feel of her.

He watched himself from different angles in the four large mirrors.

And what did he see?

He saw the *je ne sais quoi* lips of Angelina Jolie.

The Lancôme-peel glow of Christy Turlington.

The transparent complexion of Sofia Coppola.

The timeless smile of Cate Blanchett.

Enigmatic, porcelain-skinned, timeless and extraordinary.

Feline, charismatic, elegant and quirky.

He was indecently voluptuous.

A domestic goddess.

Statuesque and mesmerizing.

Booty-shaking.

Pale and luminous, curvaceous and exquisite.

He was a vivacious *It* girl, lighting up the night.

Just look at his bone structure.

Just look at his expressive, Betty Boop eyes.

He was a G.I. pin-up, six feet tall and blossoming.

He experienced gender euphoria. He was so happy he felt crazed.

He hoiked up his skirt, ripped down his tights and masturbated furiously.

Heard his gasping in the room.

Knees gave. Pearly globules slid down the mirror.

Head hangdog, peering through his hair at his reflection: the twisted, painted face of the woman with the cock.

Feeling so empty inside, so completely wrong.

He took a deep breath.

He moved towards the walk-in wardrobe.

II

HE HEARD A NOISE in the flat. A clatter, a distinct bang. He sat up in bed and listened, the liquid pulse of his heart intensifying. He heard wind whistling along the window ledge; heard a distant tram shunting softly towards Victoria. He climbed out of bed and tiptoed over to the bathroom door. He filled his lungs,

— Hello?

His voice hurt. It sounded ridiculous.

He took two fast, shallow breaths, opening the door quickly. The window rattled in the wind.

INPUT leads to PERCEPTUAL CODING.
PERCEPTUAL CODING leads to STIMULUS
    RESPONSE CONNECTION.
PERCEPTUAL CODING also leads to and from the
    MEMORY FORMATION SYSTEM.
MEMORY FORMATION SYSTEM leads to
    ASSOCIATIVE MEMORY STORE . . .
I'll never fucking understand any of it! Exclamation!
WHO are the WHITE COATS? WHO wouldn't they let
    him see?

THERE WAS SURPRISE in her voice and he thought she'd changed her mind. But no – she suggested they meet on the Curry Mile for a meal before the party. And though he knew he shouldn't – though he knew he wasn't *ready* ready for a date (and, he told himself, it probably wasn't even a *date* date anyway) – he couldn't help feeling pre-date nervous.

But he needed some friends. He needed to get out there and find some, because they sure as hell weren't beating down his door.

Friends, he kept telling himself. Remember friends?

He put on 'Bigmouth Strikes Again' and spent ages trying different jeans/shirt combinations and then he wrestled with his hair. It was so eighties, so Metal, but it hid his sticky-out ears and looked so much better than any of his wigs. Then he showered and blew a kiss at the blurred figure in the steamed-up mirror.

— Wish me luck!

JADE WAS LOOKING totally delish. She even had on a touch of make-up, subtle, not too O.T.T. He knew from experience not to comment. And there was no hiding it: he found her stunning. If you looked up the word 'gorgeous' in the dictionary, he thought.

After the curry they went to the party in Fallowfields. It was like any other full-on house party, apart from a) the music was so loud the decibels hurt your skull, and b) everyone was signing. The hearers had to sit outside, and even then they had to sit very close to each other and shout.

Antony managed some sketchy BSL with Jade's brother, John. Jade looked suitably impressed.

She rolled a small tight J and went,

— Should we try to find some pills?

He produced the three he had left over from his visit to his dealer, scoring many Jade points. He gave her one and thought briefly about his M and whether or not he should be drinking and drugging on antidepressants, but then he thought fuck it, I'm not depressed, and boshed one.

So began a lot of sighing, jaw-grinding, a lot of super-earnest chat. Human contact – he'd almost forgotten what it felt like. A wave of compassion and joyfulness spread from somewhere deep inside his brain and flowed down past his ears and across his shoulders and down his spine.

They talked about the towers and then holidays and travel. They talked about the summer's race riots and then their favourite cities (Antony's: Warsaw; Jade's: San Francisco). They discussed their favourite authors (Jade: Murakami; Antony: Kafka). They discussed their dream jobs and dream lives. Jade was a veggie; Antony an omnivore. She asked him what star sign he was and he lied and told her he was a Libra and she said yes, she knew it. But then she asked about his ex. He said the word *Rebecca* and laughed to himself. He told her he really needed to dance.

They both stuck their earplugs in and went inside.

At one point she hugged him tightly and mouthed something like,

— I'm so glad I met you.

He could feel his entire being pulsing and tingling with chemical love, but her shape, smaller and more petite than Rebecca, didn't seem to fit. He was still haunted by the ghost of Rebecca's touch, as if she'd left an invisible imprint, a mould of herself against him. Jade's small body, the smell of smoke and shampoo in her hair, the hard whorl of her ear glancing against his lips – it made his eyes sting. He knew he wanted her and didn't want to let her go, but she held him at arm's length and gave him a wounded look.

She could feel it inside.

Smiling dopily, he shrugged her off, unable to match her tone.

She had that teenage madness to her that was so infectious and insatiable but scary to be around, and she was very keen on them both getting a lift back to hers, to continue.

He told her it was nothing personal.

HE WALKED the full length of Oxford Road, stopping outside the Palace Hotel to relive the scene from *A Taste of Honey*, The Smiths' 'Reel Around the Fountain' looping round his head. In the non-hour of twilight, the Victorian Waterhouse splendour of the city centre appeared eerie and soulless, and walking through the Northern Quarter, feet aching, the prospect of Cheetham Hill suddenly seemed like Everest.

He'd jump the first tram home.

Victoria was dotted with piss-heads dozing and E-heads swaying to internal beats. He sat in the PHOTO-ME booth to keep warm, and then wandered along the platform.

The sun started to come up, and as light dappled the new

glass tower blocks in the city centre he remembered poaching with Eddie in the pre-dawn light. He remembered giant waxy leaves boomeranging back into his face and how Sonny kept nosing the back of his legs.

EDDIE TOOK the wicker box from his waist, sitting on it with a grizzled sigh. For a moment the sky paled in the moonlight and Antony saw how the valley ran in smooth waves, like a pair of cupped hands waiting for the moon to fall.

The Blue Hour. It was Eddie's favourite time of day. The hour before dawn when everything seemed to be suspended, waiting for the frost to be made.

Suddenly the rifle was in Antony's lap. The gravity of it shocked him. He could just make out the whites of Eddie's eyes as he said something about ricochets, about carrying a loaded rifle, about the safety catch never being enough.

Antony's hands began to shake.

Afterwards, Eddie laid the quarry out on the grass. An odour came from the corpses, thick and dark. Eddie hadn't told him that rabbits screamed. He hooked most of them to his waist and let Antony carry the rest. They were still warm, and with each twitch of their legs Antony's stomach hitched. He trailed Eddie, biting his bottom lip, watching the silhouette of Eddie moving into the morning light, framed by the pine trees.

He knew he'd never forget that image. That wild image.

A WEEK OF INSOMNIA- and nightmare-free sleep, and the duvet that usually caused him so much torment felt electric against his ultra-sensitized skin. His heart raced madly and jaw ached dully as techno continued to thump through his bones. He ran his hands over his tingling body, rolling around in the bed, feeling only half in this world. Tugging languorously beneath the bed sheets, surging in and out of a chemical stupor, he imagined he was being smothered by Jade's all-consuming warmth, all-consuming softness, all-consuming womanliness.

The M began to drag him under.

KENNETH'S HOUSE WAS IN complete darkness. He rang the bell and knocked on the door again, then he phoned the Centre to see if there had been any messages from Lizzie. Nothing. So he phoned the landline and listened to it ringing through the back door. He sat on their doorstep, waiting.

> RETROGRADE AMNESIA: Loss of ability to retrieve pre-
> viously stored memory.
> Kenneth's cognitive functioning assessment shows that he
> has not learnt any new vocabulary since 1995, but he is of
> superior intelligence, with an IQ of 143 and an estimated
> vocabulary of 100,000 words. His frontal executive abili-
> ties, language and deductive-reasoning skills are in the
> superior range . . .

CHEAPER SOUNDS. One of the younger lads was on the till and there was a certain hesitancy in his eyes, which Antony read as 'knowing something'. The lad was about to speak when the manager appeared and Antony was shooed out of the place like an errant shoplifter. When he got back to the Centre the manageress didn't say anything about him being late, though she did have the most infuriating of smirks on her face.

The world, he felt, was in cahoots.

ALL AFTERNOON, Antony looked around him at the abstract humans, the afflicted, the mentally challenged; the less able-bodied, the disfigured, the partially destroyed. Those who are invisible, ignored, brushed to one side. Those who are drugged up 24/7, who have electrodes on their spines to block the pain. Those whose skulls, brains, arms, legs, minds, senses are absent. Those who have led a productive life and then something happens: an accident, MS, a failed suicide attempt or just some humdrum aggressive fucker of a disease. Those who curl themselves back into a helpless, useless foetus. But they smile, they laugh, they take the piss out of each other.

Ciphers of triumph, they get on with it.

Because they've passed their test in life with flying colours.

He wasn't in the mood for 'teaching' art, so he suggested they watched a video and received a few gurgled yeses in reply. They decided to watch *Terminator*. He pressed play and turned the lights off, listening to phlegm rattling in Lerch's throat, to Derek's heavy asthmatic wheeze, to the soporific click-click-click of Maureen's MS leg tapping against her wheelchair.

Antony closed his eyes and saw two women pointing at his naked body, laughing. They tied his hands behind his back and began to punish him with the spikes of their six-inch heels. Walking on him, spitting on him, hitting him, kicking him. Then they gagged him.

He opened his eyes. Felt so at home.

LUNGING FROM A NIGHTMARE, he inhaled sharply. She was standing at the foot of his bed, her back turned. Eyes wide and fingers grasping, he made a noise. Please. But she twisted into the darkness and was gone. He stared into her absence, rubbing his wet face. Snotty, sleepy weepings. How long had it been? He climbed out of bed and stood in moonlight coming through the window, staring at his figure in a mirror, part shadow, part light. Behind him, a frowsy wig hung from a chair. He put his face to the mirror, nose flattened white, eyes the colour of fresh bruises.

— Please, he whispered. Please.

One of the carers said they were covering for him that afternoon.

— Why?

— You better check your pigeonhole.

A letter there:

Emergency meeting today

Re: Kenneth Monahan

Occupational Therapist's Office, 2 p.m.

The manageress wasn't around and no one seemed to know anything and so he went into the toilet, hit the hand drier and let it all go in a wail of FUCKs.

Think, he told himself.

He opted to take the morning's computer session and began searching the Net.

He got to the O.T.'s department just before 2:00 and found Kenneth sitting in the waiting room with a carer Antony hadn't met before.

Kenneth looked at Antony, then at the carer, and lowered his head.

Antony knocked on the O.T.'s door and walked in. The room was thick with smiles missing eyes, self-conscious coughs and averted glances. Everyone was there: Kenneth's social worker, psychologist, physiotherapist, a rep from the Primary

Care Trust, the O.T., and Lizzie looking guilty as hell with a man Antony was introduced to as her counsellor.

The manageress began the meeting in her inimitable way.

— M-m-maybe we c-could start with you, Antony? Why don't you t-tell the team how you're g-g-g-getting on, and how well the aides-memoires are are are working?

She knew fine well the aides-memoires weren't working because the rest of the care team weren't using them. Yet she put him on the spot.

— I've been researching the latest compensatory technologies available, he said. There are a lot of new, cost-effective strategies I feel we could, and should, be trying. For example, I think we need to introduce more cognitive prostheses into Kenneth's daily routine.

Without a hint of sarcasm, the O.T. asked,

— Are you a neuropsychologist?

Antony focused on his notes.

— I'm talking about simple, computer-mediated cueing aids. Kenneth's main problem is with where, how, and when to perform particular tasks. An alarm clock doesn't tell Kenneth why it's ringing. People, especially carers, are unreliable. If Kenneth can't see it, it's forgotten. Notes don't alert him to anything. He forgets to write in his diary and then he forgets to look. The calendar doesn't speak, and he's embarrassed by the labels all over the house. I feel he needs a PDA . . .

Someone sighed heavily.

— Or better still, there's a pager made by NeuroPage that Kenneth could clip to his belt. It has a flashing diode and buzzes and makes a loud chirping sound that would alert Kenneth to a simple screen message such as: GET DRESSED or MAKE BREAKFAST. The messages can be customized . . . and . . . he's learnt and retained basic computer skills . . . so . . . I know we can . . .

— But you have no formal training in this, do you?

Antony shrugged. They all looked at each other as if to say told you so.

— In the last three three three years Kenneth's p-progress has been neg-neg-negligible.

— That's not true, he said. Kenneth's learning new strategies. This is a major . . .

The looks confirmed his suspicions.

— With the c-c-current staff situation at the Day Centre, and n-n-no discernible prog-progress being made with Kenneth, I'm afraid Antony's outreach work will have to to to cease.

The counsellor put a hand on Lizzie's shoulder and went,

— And with Kenneth's behaviour last Friday [everyone glared at Antony] and his continuing aggression towards Lizzie and Sarah.

— Listen, Antony said. Kenneth *has* started remembering things. Last Friday . . .

— Last F-F-Friday you were in the pub!

— He told me he'd remembered something.

Antony looked at Lizzie.

— He must have said something? About the white coats?

Lizzie examined her hands and Antony remembered the bruises on her arms and realized he was being railroaded into agreeing that Kenneth would be better off in full-time care, and that his current funding would be better spent on more worthy causes.

Antony stormed out and approached Kenneth in the waiting room.

— Kenneth, what's my name?

The carer stood up. Antony was shaking.

— Kenneth, *what's* my name?

HE WEPT on the bus, admitting to himself that he was acting like someone who was seriously depressed. When he got home he phoned Jade. He needed someone to listen to all of this, but it diverted straight to answerphone. Then he wanted to phone Lizzie, to plead with her to wait. It'll put him back years if he goes into care. It'll ruin his recovery for good. But he couldn't.

One message keeps coming through loud and clear: STRUCTURE REDUCES ANXIETY.

He couldn't help feeling he was to blame.

HE STOOD BEFORE THE montage of women's faces, searching for a glimmer of her. He knew it wasn't a dream; that brief snapshot of a female form twisting, retwisting into darkness. He'd worn the fantasy of her like a disguise for years, the daydream him in mascara and lippy smudge. He'd tried finding her in magazines, in women on the street, remembering how they used to dance on the moors in the Blue Hour, how as a child he imagined she took the beatings for him, and yet he'd tried so hard to get rid of her. Drink, drugs, asphyxiation, his three lost years in black-and-white. But she was always there, lippy in hand, in the between places. Inside every dry urge hidden under bed sheets. She smelled of him, tasted of him, she walked through his skin and danced in his shadow. Her hands were golden flowers blooming, fingers unfurling behind his eyelids as he slipped into that moment between life and death. She helped him fight, keeping him suspended until he was released, till he silenced the sibilant sound, gasping like a newborn, fingers scratching.

He used to imagine her as a young girl in a blue-and-white gingham dress, hula-hooping and skipping, playing counting games in a street where it was always playtime. Her braided hair was full of sunshine and the air about her filled with laughter. His mother would call her in and sit her on her lap, brushing her braids out before bedtime.

Hanging in his closet, dancing in the sparks as life flickers off and on, her gingham dress would go up in flames and her laughter fade, leaving him gasping.

For it all to make sense.

For some kind of reconciliation with himself.

Whoever that was.

HE WAS CONVINCED the manageress was hiding from him. He found a new rota in his pigeon hole: Centre-based, no outreach, no Kenneth, just three extra sessions a week with Derek and an impromptu meeting for his biannual review, set for that afternoon.

Great, he thought. Fuck-wit Derek.

The main reason Antony hated Derek, was this: Antony had only been working at the Centre for a couple of weeks, and as per they were hugely understaffed and so he got lumped with the new-to-him Derek for a one-to-one cookery lesson. Risk-assessment nightmare. After a few minutes of Derek's boorish interrogations and a flat refusal to do anything Antony asked of him, Derek told him he needed a number two. So they hobbled arm-in-arm along the corridor to the accessible loo and Antony helped him undo his trousers and pull his enormous brown underpants down.

— OK, Derek, I'll be just outside when you've finished. Just give me a shout.

— No. I. Need. You. Here.

So he made Antony stand and watch him do his noisy twos while he huffed and puffed, his googly Marty Feldman eyes on him.

— Finished.

The stench was unbearable. Antony could taste it. He could chew it. The air was filled with an enormous shit sandwich.

— Don't forget to wipe now, Derek.

Derek stared at him.

— I. Can't.

66

— Sorry?

— My. Arms. Are. Too. Short.

So Antony helped him to his feet, trying not to retch while attempting some small-talk. Derek shuffled himself a hundred-and-eighty-degrees until Antony had his hairy, unceremonious arse in his face. He slipped on some latex gloves and pulled a good handful of toilet paper off the wall.

Derek looked at him over his shoulder and said,

— Do. A. Good. Job.

None of this was a problem – unpleasant, yes, but this was just part of working with the shitty end of the lollipop – it's just that later that day, in the team meeting, to everyone's amusement, ha-fucking-ha, Antony found out that Derek is fully capable of wiping his own arse.

Antony had fallen for the shit-covered handshake.

THE SECRETARY, Trudy, was taking the minutes. It was the same old rigmarole with the manageress flexing her hierarchical clout. This, of course, had nothing to do with the meeting on Tuesday or the fact that she knew Antony was close to Kenneth and upset-to-fuck.

Mismanagement 101: kick them when they're down.

But at the end of the review she went,

— Where would you like to be be be in say three years' ti-time, Antony?

Without hesitation,

— Sitting where you're sitting, but doing a good job.

Trudy smiled appreciatively as she jotted it down.

As he was leaving the Centre he got a text from Jade, asking when they were going to see each other again.

He thumbed a reply but couldn't press send.

HE LISTENED to the purr of the receiver, imagining Lizzie sitting in the darkening living room, TV switched off, staring at the ringing telephone as the evening closed around her like sleep.

THE PSYCH WAS ALWAYS five or ten minutes late. He'd come into the waiting room and give Antony a solemn nod and then the two men would walk the narrow corridor in silence.

What Antony hated most about the therapy room was its sparseness: there were no paintings on the walls and the beat furniture hadn't been upgraded for at least twenty years and it was slightly too small for the lanky psych who was always fidgeting, twisting his creepy long limbs in an attempt to get comfy.

He was in his late fifties, which Antony found both reassuring – he'd obviously heard, and seen, a lot of shit over the years – but at the same time worrying – perhaps he'd become jaded by it all? (The latter would explain why the psych was frequently stifling yawns.) He had a comb-over and wore thick glasses, behind which his tiny eyes seemed to puncture you.

There were the customary few uneasy seconds while they both gawped at each other, willing the other to start.

Between them sat a box of man-sized Kleenex on a small glass-top table.

Antony decided to stop editing his thoughts.

— This might sound glib and ridiculous, he said, but just because I considered throwing myself under a train a few months back, does that necessarily mean I'm depressed? I mean, I've entertained ideas like that all my life. And these pills they prescribed me. I mean?

The psych repositioned himself and said,

— Tell me about the first time you met your father.

Antony inhaled raggedly and turned his face to the window. He recalled that journey back from the prison, the road stretching away from a relationship that had taken its first breath. How in the distance he could see the massed, snowy horizon of home, and he'd looked at those hills and they made him wonder about the space between things. He remembered the parallel lines of electricity cables running along the side of the road, extending into the distance where everything appeared to meet, and it felt as if his life was going in reverse.

As if his life was a constant process of retreat.

A FEW HOURS LATER, he found himself standing in his tiny kitchen, staring blindly into the cutlery drawer. The sessions with the psych – he wondered what was going to happen, and why he felt like he was describing someone else's life. He knew there would be a time when he'd have to tell the psych about what he did in the wardrobe, about the woman who slid in and out of his life, about the girl crying in the room next door, except there was no room next door. And what happened, he wondered, if he unravelled himself so completely there was nothing left.

He picked a large knife out of the drawer. His reflection along the blade: distorted, cambered. He ran his thumb lightly over the serrated edge, remembering how the tree had shivered nervously in the wind outside the therapy room window.

He inhaled sharply, dropping the knife, sucking the ferric-tasting blood from his thumb, and moved over to the window. The city outside, cloaked in a drab grey fog that smothered the neon and streetlights.

He squeezed his thumb.

Smeared blood across the glass.

THE WELCOME SURPRISE of Lizzie's voice.

— I just wanted to know, she said. Would you come with me tomorrow?

He moved his face back into the light above the mirror.

— Where?

— The unit. Where Kenneth. Where he's going to be . . .

Static clicked and clacked down the line as she paused.

Antony tapped the brush on the lid, blending the powder above his left eye in a concentric motion towards the brow-bone.

— Lizzie?

— Sorry.

— Will Kenneth be coming with us?

— No, he won't.

Antony turned his back on his reflection and listened to her breathe.

— Are you OK?

— No, she said. I'm not.

— So when will Kenneth be moving to the unit?

She swallowed audibly, then said quietly,

— Next week.

Quick work, Antony thought.

— Give me the address, he said. I'll meet you there.

HE SCREWED THE HOOK-EYES in and tied the keys, passing
the cordage and chain over the clothes pole, hands moving in
a fluid, intuitive performance.

He could almost have been sleepwalking again.

He rammed the lacy knickers into his mouth and pulled
some low-deniers over his head, fastening them with a studded
leather choker.

He smiled. He knew how hideous it made him look.

Then he stood on the chair and padlocked, hooked, looped,
and threaded. Then he hooked and looped again, and then
snapped the heavy padlock shut beneath his hair.

One more pass, one more turn, terminating at his wrists.

He hesitated for a second, but didn't padlock it.

Dead Man's Release.

With a thrust of his head, he yanked the closet door closed.
Heard the final lock SNAP.

In the darkness he saw the smudged colours, the green sparks
ranging behind his eyes as his heart punched its liquid Morse.

His toes began their excited waggle, anticipating the hangman's dance.

He smelt his own sweet sweat and felt the silent lull.

She was almost there.

He moved forwards, feeling the edges of the chair with his
toes,

and slowly, slowly,
let his feet
slide
o
f
f
.

SHE BREATHES FOR HIM. He travels so far the planet becomes a periwinkle iris in a black void, and every star is a woman hanging in the sky. She helps him leave, and when he slips into that moment between life and death it's like drowning, like falling into the deepest of sleeps and he never wants to wake. But she helps him fight in his closet, kicking out wildly, blindly. She dances in the sparks, and the flower that blooms before his eyes are her hands unfurling as she holds him there, suspended, until he's released. That invisible line that led him into the night – it got caught around his neck. Dancing in the colours that range behind his eyes, dancing in the sibilant sound that fills his skull, her body lit up in sparklight as his life flickers off and on.

She holds him there.

She holds him.

III

SPARKLE HAPPINESS
SUNSHINE GRINNING
POWERFUL LOVING
GLITTERING EXCITING
RICHNESS RADIANT
CHEEKY BLISS LAUGHTER
HILARIOUS JOYFUL
EXUBERANT SENSUOUS
VIBRANT BEAUTIFUL
HARMONY YOU!

HE GOT UP AT 7:00 a.m. and drew the curtains and put U2's 'Beautiful Day' on the stereo. Like the psych told him: no more of The Smiths or Joy Division or Nine Inch Nails to rouse himself to. After two months, he believed he could feel something in his brain being rewired, the M simultaneously blocking his alpha$_2$ receptors while provoking his 5HT$_2$ and 5HT$_3$ receptors.

These facts, they gave him such a hard-on.

He went and stood in front of the bathroom mirror and smiled at himself, reciting the list of words he and the psych had compiled together, scrawled across the bathroom mirror in the hottest vermilion lipstick. They were meant to help him triumph over the blueprint that had so far steered his life:

A lack of confidence;
Eating too little;
Tasmanian devil nutter moments;
Hopelessness;
Self-centredness;
Excessive drinking and drugging;
Having his head stuck up his own arse;
Not being able to enjoy life;
Being unable to share;
A total lack of concentration;

Inability to be anything resembling a friend;
His fucked-up circadian rhythms;
Wanking ten times a day like a caged chimpanzee;
And feeling, generally, quite manky inside.

So his daily introduction to himself was now fortified with constructive, affirmative feelings – words, floating before his reflected face, which he recited at the top of his lungs while smiling beatifically. Yeah!

But every word he'd written on the mirror was a word he'd use to describe the experience of hanging himself for kicks.

He had yet to tell the psych this.

HE THOUGHT they had everything sorted. Just platonic, you know. Besides, she knew getting tangled up with him would be emotional suicide. But when he hugged Jade goodbye at the station that day, she moved her head and fleetingly, clumsily, their lips glanced. It was hardly dry-humping, tonsil-tickling, nipple-tweaking action right there on the platform, but he pulled away and she looked, well: crestfallen. This constant to-and-froing between them – he knew there'd be a point when she'd get sick of it. Who'd blame her? She could have had anyone she wanted. Anyone. He should've gone back to hers. Should've Gone-With-The-Moment.

But he couldn't and didn't know why.

HE WAS in the middle of showing Derek and Lerch how to make butterfly cakes – such a valuable Independent Living skill – when Derek beckoned him.

— Antony?

— What?

— Come. Here. Closer.

Antony thought that Derek was trying, for once, to be discreet about the sudden smell in the room, of Lerch filling his nappy.

Antony put his ear next to Derek's mouth and Derek whispered,

— Wanker.

Behind him came the sound of choking as Lerch set in motion his version of laughter. Then Derek started. Then Antony started. The three of them laughing as Derek began a long, staccato fart, like the sound-effect from a horror movie.

At times like these Antony loved his job.

Belly aching, he pushed Lerch out into the corridor.

HIS PROGRESS in the sessions over the first two months could be summarized thus: he circled, he span, he skirted, he sidestepped. There were hours of either non-stop shit-talk or staring into the Blank Indeterminate Place. Usually the psych just sat there, lanky limbs twined in the too-small chair and that expression on his face: opaque. Antony viewed their doctor-patient relationship thus: the taxpayer was paying the psych to allow Antony to lay steaming turds into his expansive, shit-container head.

— Tell me what to do with all of this stuff inside of me.

He blurted it all out and for what? To hear his own voice bouncing off the walls.

Then, out of the blue, the psych said it.

— There'll be a time in the future when you'll need to speak to her.

He meant his mother.

— To get closure.

He told the psych to go fuck himself and slammed the door behind him.

THE WHITE COATS. Is this a FLASHBULB MEMORY?
Is it REAL? Could this serve as a cue to retrieve further
biographical information?
Have I found a way in?

HE GOT TO the unit twenty minutes earlier than his allotted
visiting time of noon. He wanted to meet Lizzie on her way
out. To catch up.

When he visited the unit with Lizzie that first time, he
thought I wouldn't be surprised if they had an electroshock
room. The place was like a prison, total Cuckoo's Nest. Lizzie
said nothing but Antony could see it in her eyes: one hundred
per cent guilt.

Kenneth had been living there for two weeks by now. They
said he was having trouble 'getting settled' – hence this was
Antony's first proper visit to see him, and he was hoping
Kenneth hadn't forgotten his name.

As he walked towards the front gate, he saw Lizzie getting
into a car. He shouted at her but she didn't seem to hear.
That's when he saw the man behind the wheel. Lizzie put
her head down as they drove on by. When Antony looked
back towards the unit, he saw Kenneth at an upstairs window,
staring down into the front garden, forehead pressed against
the glass. He must've seen. He must. But he would have

forgotten as soon as he saw it. An after-burn of anger he didn't understand.

Antony was shown to Kenneth's room.

Kenneth looked grizzled, unkempt, drawn. Salt and pepper speckled stubble, clothes stale, stinking. He gave Antony a look of recognition but refused to meet his eye.

Antony noticed there were no labels on the doors or cupboards. No wall chart, no informational hub.

Antony stepped towards him and said,

— What's my name?

Kenneth replied flatly,

— Leave me alone.

HE ASKED to see Kenneth's key worker. She took him into her office.

— Why isn't Kenneth shaved?

— He's taking longer to adjust than we expected. Nothing to worry about.

She coughed falsely. Her breath was a wave of fish.

— We're used to aggressive clients, but Kenneth's language?

— Fuck Kenneth's language, it's his well-being I care about. What about his aides-memoires? His Care Plan?

— We've started using the file you've put together. Believe me, we have highly trained staff here. We'll do everything we can to assist Kenneth.

— How many times has Lizzie been to see him? Is this, like, respite forever?

— She comes every Saturday morning without fail.

— And Sarah?

The woman looked over his shoulder.

— Sarah refuses to come.

HE FOUND KENNETH watching a huge television with a group of about twenty residents in the Leisure Room. The television was deafeningly loud and no one spoke or looked at each other and no one seemed to register Antony was there.

Antony saw the upright piano against a wall. He crouched beside Kenneth.

— Have you had a go on the piano yet? Fancy knocking off a tune?

Kenneth looked at him slowly and mouthed silently,

— Fuck. Off.

On the bus home, Antony watched the streets rolling by, thinking about Kenneth in that place at night, alone with his slippery ruminations, wondering where Lizzie is and why he's in that shit-hole in the first place.

Kenneth didn't know that man had walked on the moon or that the Vietnam War was over or that the Berlin Wall had been torn down. He didn't know about Live Aid, Bloody Sunday, the poll-tax riots, the Guildford Four, the Hyde Park bombings, the Lockerbie disaster, the euro or Blair's landslide victory. He didn't even know that Jimi Hendrix and Janis Joplin and John Lennon and Elvis Presley were dead, or that scientists had cracked DNA and cloned one ugly fucking sheep. But Antony was certain Kenneth *was* aware that he *was not* at home, that he *did not* wake up to Lizzie every morning, and that his memory loss *was to blame*.

He pictured Kenneth walking figure-of-eights.

THE BUS LEFT TODMORDEN train station and snaked its way
up onto 'the tops', driving through amber moorland that
sparkled beneath the bright emptiness of the evening sky.
Jade's village was the final stop, an ancient clutter of black
stone cottages and slippery cobbled streets. He found the
graveyard where Jade said Sylvia Plath was buried and headed
towards a long row of terraced houses. He stopped to check
the map she'd drawn and heard a tapping noise coming from
a window.

She opened the front door.

— Now then, he said.

She squinted at him.

— Now then *what*?

They hugged tightly. She recoiled, frowning.

— You stink of perfume.

— It's close-contact work.

He said it too quickly and it surprised him.

— I either smell of perfume or shit, he added. Which
would you prefer?

He followed her inside, the Morse of his heart beating liar,
liar, liar.

The house had been newly refurbished: treated wooden
beams and exposed stonework and a fancy modern kitchen of
brushed-stainless steel, and what looked to Antony's eyes like

85

pricey walnut floors. But every room was filled with the pervasive after-stench of veggie cooking and joss sticks.

— My flatmate's just gone to the offie. She's looking forward to meeting you.

Antony wondered what Jade had told her.

They entered a large, attic bedroom, and Antony scanned Jade's open wardrobe, the array of cosmetics on her dressing table. He felt a judder of excitement.

She opened the Velux window and they looked out over the barren moors.

— It's amazing, he said, what you get on benefits nowadays.

She elbowed him.

— The lowest form of wit.

They stood beside each other, looking out beyond the graveyard towards a mill on a distant hillside. He listened to her breathing beside him; soft sounds coming from soft lips. It was such a pure moment and he felt an overwhelming urge to embrace her, but he made a stupid joke and they went back downstairs.

Jade's flatmate had returned with a few skanky, weirdy-beardy friends. Three of them had guitars and one had a pair of bongos. Antony groaned inwardly.

They clocked him straight away for being a bit older, a lot 'straighter', certainly better dressed and definitely in gainful employment, but as soon as he pulled out the bag of goodies he'd procured from his dealer, well, quelle surprise, they suddenly wanted to talk to him.

— Hey man, so where you from?

— Hey dude, got any skins?

He did a sneaky-pete double-drop and watched the night break.

HALF-SENTENCES and splintered dialogue, tales unfinished amid earnest drivel, cigarettes hanging off lips, people on pause, over-the-top laughter and paranoid whats? A few huddled deranged in the kitchen, high on absinthe. The world looks like a Van Gogh painting, one of them said. Jade sat cross-legged in front of her flatmate, their foreheads touching as they talked.

Antony wandered up the stairs and back into her empty bedroom. He examined the make-up on her dressing table. A few Lancôme and Boots items – that was all.

Here's a girl lucky enough not to need much make-up.

He sat on her bed and began building a J, tuning into the sounds of laughter coming from downstairs, surprised by Jade's voice in the room,

— Having a good snoop, are we?

He was momentarily hypnotized by the way she moved across the room. She put some music on the stereo and then switched on the twinkling fairy lights that train-tracked the ceiling. Hitting the main light, she sank the room into a shifting pattern of reds and greens, and then she let the soft night air fall in through the window.

She approached him, slightly crouched, hands clapping, smiling beatifically.

— You being anti-social?

He wanted to be inside her. Wanted her skin.

— Just needed a break from them all.

— I know what you mean.

She sat next to him on the bed, rolling a cigarette between her fingers.

They sat like that for some time, saying nothing, moving slowly to the beat, shoulders touching as Antony felt that uncanny warmth spread inside his stomach and across his chest. He passed her the J and watched her smoke with her eyes closed.

He reminded himself where he was: amid Jade's things. The bed she slept in. The couch where she watched TV. The shower where she touched herself. He wondered how many times thoughts of him had entered these intimate spaces. Did she think about him as much as he thought about her? In the same way? In bed with the lights off before sleep.

Her body in his mind. His mind in her body.

She coughed, breaking the reverie. Her gorgeous big black irises bloomed.

She asked him about his time at art college and he sighed slowly. He danced his fingers across his tingling scalp, the feel of his long hair sending shivers down his arms. He experienced a sudden moment of voluble clarity.

He told her how he'd lived for the weekends, for that smorgasbord of E and beak and dance, how they were living outside of time, outside of any external narrative, about how you become a lump of meat carrying a brain around, a brain stimulated to the max, because what else is there? Yes you jam the pleasure button, press and press for hours, for days, until the world fully recedes and the brain can take no more, and you become totally insensate, listening to the world like a coma victim because there's nothing else in this world that releases you from yourself and from the narrative within.

She laughed,

— You fucking weirdo.

He became a swirling, whirling, stirring, a swelling of soft tissue, a weakening, a blood-flow, a slackening of self. King of shite-talk.

She crinkled her cute nose and put her head in his lap.

He went,

— Let's stick some different music on, eh?

So they ended up at the window again with Underworld blaring away and he was wondering what it'd feel like to hold her naked.

She looked at him all moony, swallowing slowly as if buying time, and went,

— Why have I never met any of your friends?

He shrugged.

— And why do you never talk about your family?

88

— I don't have any family, he said.

— Course you do.

— None that matter.

— And how come you've never invited me to your flat?

— Come whenever you want. You don't need an invite.

His voice sounded like a replica.

— Anyway, he said, I hate people that talk about themselves all the time.

He gestured towards the skanks downstairs. She made a *hrmm* noise and sighed slowly, jaw jutting, eyes far away.

Then she asked about Rebecca.

— Look, it still hurts, he said. That's why you and me. That's why I want us to get to know each other first. People rush into these things. I'm so glad I met you.

He went in for a hug but she held him back.

— 'These things'? *This* can be whatever *we* want it to be.

She put her hands to his face, her moist eyes dipping and flaring as she said,

— Should we do another pill?

He didn't get it. She was a total fucking stunner and any man in his right mind. He loved her smell, her words, her voice, her thoughts, her movements, and these things only made friendship with her even more intense and he never wanted it to stop, but the pervasive fear of rejection still existed. She seemed protected by some benevolent force he couldn't contend with. He wanted to tell her: I'll fuck you up, I'll drive you crazy, I'll let you down. You'll rapidly grow sick of my face. You'll hate every subtle nuance that makes up Antony Dobson. And you'll only ever know the half of me.

But when he was with her, it felt like his consciousness was being raised.

That warmth in his body, the first tingles of love – they scared him.

So he gave her another pill hoping that she'd fall off time, but when the skanks downstairs eventually staggered home she told him not to be so fucking soft, he could share her bed.

— You won't get a cab round here this time of night.

— I'll kip on the couch.

— Don't be a knob.

He went to the bathroom and ran a tap and tried to empty his balls, but he remained flaccid. Then he was undressing beneath the glow of the fairy lights and slipping between her cold bed sheets, wondering which side he should lie on, worried she'd see the shrunken, lifeless chipolata in his underpants.

He sniffed the faint smell of her hair on her pillow, thinking how tonight was so unlike any other: those bedrooms, objects, memories, routines. Those leftover moments from other relationships. He knew this was different; it was brand new.

WALKING TOWARDS HIM through the bedroom dark, a slat of light illuminated her peek-a-boo nightgown, and a brief snapshot of her breasts that made him ache. She climbed in beside him, French knickers revealing the tight curves of her perfect white arse, smiling coyly.

— I won't bite, she said.

He opened his arms and she snuggled into him. His heart was beating so loud he was sure the entire village could hear it thumping through the mattress.

She leaned on an elbow, tucking her hair behind her ears.

— We don't have to have sex, she said, running a fingernail the length of his arm. But I'd really like to.

Antony stared inward.

— I don't want you to think I'm a slut or anything, she said. I mean, just because I like sex. I think about it a lot. Not just with you, but with other men. I imagine them undressing me. Touching me.

Her lips parted with a burst of air. Unbidden the word *quief* popped into his head.

— I hope you don't mind, she said. I thought I could talk to you.

He swallowed dryly.

— You can tell me anything.

— I was fifteen when I first tried. But I couldn't do it. There was something wrong with my muscles, you know. Down there.

She made an oblique gesture with her fingers.

— I just couldn't open up. As much as I wanted to. Just couldn't.

— That must've been . . . hard.

She barked a deep, dark laugh.

— But I'm wet now, she said. And I want you.

— I can't.

She dropped her head heavily onto the pillow, holding her breath for a long time.

— It's the drugs, he said quickly. I couldn't even if . . .

She placed a hand on his hip.

— I can help you.

— Look, this might sound lame, but I just want to hold you.

She moved so gently into his arms she felt weightless. He kissed the top of her head, inhaling the safe smell of her scalp.

I don't want to be like this any more, he told himself.

He held her until she began sleep-breathing, and then he slipped out of bed and slept on the floor beside her.

BLUE LIGHT SLICED through the edges of the Velux blind, mixing with the remnants of a dream that felt more like a memory: one patent black stiletto positioned over his throat, the cold thin heel pressing against his neck as the woman above him slowly parted her legs.

Jade was sleeping with her face to the wall, so still her body seemed lifeless. He watched her to make sure she was breathing, and then he crept from the house, remembering

91

her ghostly figure walking across the room towards him last night.

He let himself out into the new morning light.

The distant moorland shimmered like beaten copper.

HE CHECKED his Hotmail account. Just a slew of the usual spam.

```
$1500 Overnight Cash Advance for You!
RolexSale
hungLikeAHorse
Someone wants to date you
Meet Hot Single Latinas
Lets ScrewOur Brains Out
```

He opened the 'Rebecca' file and looked at the first email she ever sent him, thinking, do I feel the same way about Rebecca then as I feel about Jade now?

```
It was great to talk to you last night. I'm
really glad that you would like to go out at the
weekend. It will be lovely to see you.
Was grilled about you by my two flatmates last
night on my return to the flat! They're looking
forward to meeting you properly soon.
I'm so glad that we both want to see each other
again. I feel very excited about getting to
know you better.
Speak to you soon sweetheart
X X X
```

When you're so used to bouncing around life on your own, a body beside you can feel like love. It can make the nights seem sweet and the days almost bearable. He was so intrigued by Rebecca's behaviour, her movements, her speech, mimicking them in his head. She'd catch him looking and it cut him up, because he realized he wanted to be her. Wondering about the days ahead, burying his face into her hair, whispering soft-mouthed into her ear. But it was just infatuation. Infatuation with her breasts. Infatuation with her eyes. Infatuation with her skin. Infatuation with her cunt. The way she moved. The sounds she made. He was plain jealous.

And closing his eyes, he was suddenly back in Greece again.

It was meant to be a time to rekindle, a new beginning. Lying on the beach watching old couples rubbing cream into their coffee-coloured skin – chance memories like these skittered though his skull as he opened his eyes and stared at the final Xs of her email. Kiss kiss kiss.

He inhaled deeply. Held his breath.

A dog riding on the back of a motorbike.

Bright terraces of pastel-hued bougainvillea, pawed by a sea breeze.

A boy lifting his face from the volcanic black sand, his cheek like peppered steak.

And Rebecca's body, oiled, turning to tan, her pulse flickering in the hollow of her neck where the collarbones meet and dip. Lying on her back in her skimpy red bikini, her legs opening and closing like a butterfly warming in the sun.

Like the one tattooed onto the small of her back.

He remembered the breeze coming in off the sea, lifting gooseflesh and making her nipples crease, pushing against the damp fabric of her bikini. He had to look away.

On the mountainside, the land had been farmed right to the edges of the cliffs, and he imagined a farmer up there, sitting in his garden at dusk, watching the westering sun, sky turning the colour of Fanta Orange.

It was hot-hot, like the summers when he was a kid. Local boys whined by on tinnitus mopeds, short and stocky in their tight white T-shirts, the roily sheen of their curly black hair.

A child screamed.

A man walked out of the sea pulling at the front of his shorts.

A woman lifted one of her heavy breasts, looking at the skin beneath.

A man held a cigarette in one hand, a book in the other.

And Rebecca's silences mounted like heavy stones.

And in the afternoons, when everything seemed to stop, he thought about his old suitcase back at home, wondering when the woman in the mirror would next make an appearance.

He thought Rebecca was the cure. Maybe he'd get it down to just once or twice a year. She might not be over the moon about it, but she'd see the need in him and let him because it made him whole. But as soon as she found the suitcase and make-up box, the gulf began to widen. So he told her he'd throw them all away, put an end to it, once and for all. He suggested a holiday: my treat.

One night, alone on the beach, curling his toes into wet sand, he saw shapes out at sea: people night swimming. And out across that very same sea, on a tiny island, Jack had made a new life for himself. A new home. A new family.

A new son.

Antony exhaled heavily, head spinning.

He didn't want to be like this any more.

HE STOOD AT HIS WINDOW, watching Manchester bloom and dim like a thousand dancing fireflies. He ran a finger along his windowsill. His flat needed a good air and dust, but after a couple of vodkas he thought what's the point? He wanted to be out there, feeding off the thrill of the city at night, but his Friday sessions with the psych always left him feeling so 2D.

There must be somebody out there feeling like me tonight.

The psych's opaque gaze was haunting. This feeling of being caught out. The contemplative shrewd nods. The excruciating silences. What Antony wanted to say was, What do you think, really? For Antony felt as if he was see-through, as if the psych could walk the rooms of his mind, torch in hand, illuminating the dark places. As if the psych could see the woman's face in his analytical laser beam, and was just waiting for Antony to introduce them both. His fantasy incarnated; it terrified him.

He was expecting a lecture about missing a week, but the psych said jack-shit.

The inscrutable eyes. The *hrmm* sound in his throat.

He was aware that the psych kept saying very little, but when he did, it shocked him. He felt as if he was being steered towards something but he didn't know what.

At one point the psych leaned across to Antony and said,

— Society incarcerated your father. Society punished you because your mother is a lesbian. Who do *you* punish, Antony?

THE HEADACHES RETURNED and so it happened again. Waves of pain and the sibilant noise that bent him double, hands to head, until he needed to get out the cordage and start preparing because it was the only way to stop the pain. He went through his finely tuned regimen, but when it came down to it, he couldn't. He had his bath and got dressed and the waves of noise just stopped. The room was full of light and he felt he was almost floating, sparks whizzing around his head.

Then silence, stillness, calm. His breath, caught.

So he sat watching TV in a floral-print dress and his make-up, just sat there en-femme, stroking the sweat from his vodka glass and feeling *ridiculously* content.

The psych's words a nagging, faint loop in his head.

HE WAS DREADING seeing Kenneth that Saturday; didn't think he could handle another hour of being ignored and told to fuck off. He got there a tad later than usual, to avoid seeing Lizzie in a car with some random bloke, but as soon as he entered the building he could hear Kenneth singing and playing his heart out.

The Leisure Room.

A handful of people sat in high-backed chairs and stared glaze-eyed, but the majority of residents were clustered around Kenneth on the piano. A woman with bird's-nest hair was whacking a tambourine against her hips and an enormous fat bloke was clapping his hands and stamping his feet, humming a bass-line.

There was a tap on Antony's shoulder. Kenneth's key worker, Nurse Bog Breath, waved at him to follow her, and as he left the Leisure Room he was sure he heard Kenneth sing, —He's a Pinball Wizard, he's got such a massive di-i-ick!

— Would you like a drink, Antony? Tea? Coffee?

— I'm fine, cheers. Kenneth's the life and soul, eh?

She took her glasses off and cleaned them methodically on the hem of her blouse.

— Isn't he just?

She sat next to him, far too close for comfort, rubbing her fingers along the pleats of her pencil-line skirt. Her teeth, he noticed, were small crenulated squares sitting inside her mouth like castle ramparts. He couldn't imagine anyone wanting to kiss that mouth.

— Has Kenneth always had such a way with language?

Antony leaned away from her.

— He has a vocabulary of 100,000 words and a genius IQ.

— I know. That's why I don't understand the constant profanities.

— A swearword used in the right place can be a very powerful thing.

— But it's non-stop.

Antony told her he thought it was Kenneth's confusion and frustration that were non-stop, and that he guessed for someone of Kenneth's intellect, swearing must be a major release valve.

— Is it an issue? You want rid of him as well?

— I just want to understand.

She squinted at him.

— You all right? Your eyes are *terribly* bloodshot.

He was taken off guard.

— Has he called you a bitch? Don't take it personally, he doesn't mean it.

He checked his watch.

— I'm going to make the most of my visit. If you'll excuse me.

KENNETH WAS in his bedroom sweating and panting. He looked ecstatic. He ran towards Antony and hugged him.

— Antony *cunting* Dobson. My bastard conscience.

With a canny expression he went over to his chest of drawers. Antony noticed the little printed signs on everything at last.

Socks and Pants.
T-shirts.
Trousers.

Kenneth pulled out a framed black-and-white photograph.

They were maybe sixteen, seventeen years old in the picture. Lizzie was wearing a long puffy dress and was sat on an old pushbike with an arm around Kenneth's shoulder. You could tell it was summertime and taken beside the sea somewhere. Kenneth had a fringed Mod hairdo and his shirtsleeves were rolled up. He looked strong and vibrant and his expression said he had the whole world in his arms: Lizzie.

Kenneth started fiddling with the photograph. He slid the cardboard off the back and tipped the glass onto the bed. Then he lifted the photo out. Secreted beneath it was another photograph. Kenneth looked at it, frowned, and then passed it to Antony.

A colour Polaroid of a young baby in a lacy pink outfit.

— I don't know, Kenneth said. Don't know who she is.

Antony shrugged.

— But I remember her being born.

— What?

— The fuss. The fucking *fuss*. Lizzie's screaming. I remember the corridor outside. It was dark, wood-panelled. Can picture it now. And the white-coat cunts, they wouldn't let me in to see her. But she got worse, you see. They thought she might die. I went fucking berserk. Ask her.

Kenneth picked up the photograph and pointed.

— I remember Lizzie's face. And her screams. Worst thing I've ever heard in my life. I thought she was a goner.

Kenneth looked startled.

— Then I remember this baby coming out. When I close my eyes, I can see it.

He clicked his fingers.

— Arse first.

He took the picture off Antony and stroked it.

— But I don't know who she is.

Then he pointed at Antony.

— What the *fuck* is wrong with your *neck*?

Memory types related to time: Immediate, also known as iconic. The sensory register, the brief period of memory after stimulation. *The warmth of her mouth, my cock unfurling in her hand . . .*
Short-term lasts for less than 1 minute. *Did they say right or left turn? Fuck. I can't remember!*
Long-term is the storage of experience, episodic memory, autobiographical.
I remember . . .

HE WAS TELLING Jade he thought Kenneth might have accessed a flash of his retrograde memory, when she stopped him – rudely, he felt – and said,
— I need to know where I stand.
Antony took the phone away from his ear and placed it on the table. He walked around the room, hands to head. He opened a drawer and stared into it. Then he picked up the phone again.
— Hello?
— I'm still here.
— I really like you, Jade. I like you a lot.
— Is that it?
— Look, you know I can't . . .
She started screaming down the phone. He heard a few

distinct FUCKs, BASTARDs, and SELFISH WANKERs before she hung up.

He paced about some more and then went to the freezer and scratched the ice from the side of a vodka bottle. He realized he needed to get out of the flat.

IT WAS WEIRD seeing the kitchen without the labels and wall planner.

Lizzie didn't offer him a drink.

— So, he said. How you getting on without him?

She stared out of the window, arms folded. Antony heard a noise upstairs, coming from her and Kenneth's bedroom. She'd taken ages to answer the door and her hair was a total mess. Sex hair, he thought to himself. Another noise made her turn to Antony.

— What do you want?

— Kenneth seems to be settling in.

She snorted,

— Really?

He wanted to shout: DON'T YOU FUCKING MISS HIM?

— How's Sarah doing? She OK?

— A lot better. Now.

— Can I ask you something?

She flashed him a worried look.

— When was Sarah born?

Hesitantly, she said,

— '83. Why?

— Was it an easy birth?

— It's never *easy*.

— Was Kenneth there?

— Course not.

She eyed him slowly.

— What's going on in that head of yours?

— Nothing.

He made his excuses and left.

LUCKILY, YOU HAVE your own fair, shoulder-length hair, and you're far from being hirsute, but you always have a bath, shave twice, and moisturize first anyway.

Then you slip tonight's outfit on and prepare your make-up, lining everything along your dresser-top: brushes; concealer; cream foundation; translucent powder; eyeshadow; mascara; blush; and liquid eyeliner.

Rimmel. Estee. Lancôme. No. 7. Clinique. Chanel.

Then you tie your hair back.

You find beiges the best for covering the Blue Jaw. You place the powder on a make-up sponge, pat it on, and then use concealer to hide the suitcases under your eyes.

A bit of loose powder on the puff fixes the first layer.

You blend the edges and place the normal foundation on over the top; Dermacolour Light; as close to your original skin tone as is possible.

Start with the forehead, and then spread across the bridge of the nose, eyebrows, ears, and under your nostrils. Blend, pat, trowel it on over the Blue Jaw. Then gently wipe over the chin, down towards the neckline and over your Adam's apple.

Clarted up, you look ghost-like.

You comb and pencil your eyebrows, thinning out the arch.

Eyeshadow. You tend to use variations of beige and light

browns between the eye and nose. It draws attention to the eyes, and it's at this stage that you think of Val.

Eyeliner. Thin point from inner eye and thicken outwards. Blend with your fingers to finish off. Then use a touch of white below the brow-bone and a bit of shadow under the eye to give it a smoky look.

Mascara. You always use a couple of coats and do the top lashes first, keeping your eyes shut for a minute to avoid clarting your eyelids. When dried, you brush the lashes out.

Blusher. You perfect that whole apple-and-cheekbone, equidistance-between-ear-and-nose-thing, that you learned from your women's magazines.

Finally the lippy. You draw in the shape with the Nude Shade lip-liner, just outside the natural line, and then colour in the lips to give them a basic foundation. Then apply the lipstick. (Val's lipstick used to extend well behind the natural lip line, which leant her face that cartoonish-look of a surprised, smeared snarl. You loved it.)

An hour later, you're ready.

IT MUST BE the tablets, he told himself, the M making me into a happy zombie, changing my circuitry, reformatting my hard drive, corrupting my libido, CTRL-Zing the need to hang. The muffled, polyphonic tones of 'Vicious' made him jump – his jacket was calling him. He stood there and stared, afraid of the noise. Then the room seemed to dim in the silence. A minute later, a solitary buzz.

He read the message.

```
mother. penmevan cottage mevagissey cornwall.
call her. jack.
```

And then a telephone number.

It felt like Jack could see him, like Jack was watching him sitting there in a pretty dress in front of the TV and laughing his fucking head off.

The words Jack would use.

Antony got into the shower and washed her from him, and then he read the text again, wondering: why?

IV

THE DAY CENTRE'S CHRISTMAS party – it was the only day of the year the staff got to kick back a little, because the clients brought either their family or other carers. Idiotically, Lerch had been administered a suppository that morning and so, much to his shambling irritation, he wasn't allowed any of the finger buffet or minging sarnies or mountains of soft crisps. But, when no one was looking, Antony sneaked some cava into his spaggy sucky cup. He managed to hold it down.

After work, Antony popped into Cheaper Sounds. The young bloke was there, the one with the bonehead, and when he saw Antony he looked all hangdog.

Poised, the boss looked at Bone Head, then Antony, as if waiting for something.

Antony went downstairs to the vinyl and cassette section. He found an early sixties compilation on cassette and went back up. Bone Head wasn't there. The manager served Antony without looking or speaking to him. Antony asked him to gift-wrap it and the manager huffed and stuck it in a shiny little box with stars on.

— Thank you so much. Do you have any cards?

The manager squinted with a just-perceptible curl of the lip before shoving a small card into the bag.

NURSE BOG BREATH intercepted him at the front door.

— Kenneth went walkabout this morning.

— Is he OK?

— He's drunk.

— Well, it *is* the festive.

— He was verbally abusive to one of our new staff members.

— And what do you want me to do about it?

She sighed.

— Try and have a word with him. He respects you.

Antony went up to Kenneth's room to find him in bed, fully clothed, snoring.

STOMACH A MESS, he pressed Jade's number.

— You have every right to be angry with me, he said quickly.

She sighed over-dramatically.

— Ah, well, I was preparing myself to forgive you anyway, arsehole.

They both said sorry and laughed at the same time.

— Really. Everything's fine?

— Shut up, soft lad. Christmas.

— What about it?

— Eileen. She told me to invite you for dinner.

— Eileen?

— My mother.

He was, quite literally, speechless.

— It'll be laid back. No pressure. There's usually a big crowd anyway. John's bringing his friend, the absurdly named Moon. You can get some signing practice in.

— Thanks, but I've made other plans.

— What's that smell? Can you smell that?

— Eh?

— Like somebody's bum's on fire.

— Am I that transparent?

— Come on, it'll be fun. They know we're only mates.

The word 'mates' was laced with a mote of resentment.

— Really, she said, what else you going to do?

He'd planned to sleep as late as possible and spend the rest of the day in a pretty dress eating pizza and watching TV while getting very stoned and *not* thinking about all the perfect little families in the world, and him, yet again, on his lonesome, feeling totally 'Heaven Knows I'm Miserable Now'.

— Look, come round for twoish. We'll have done the embarrassing presents thing and we'll be well stuck into the booze by then. Grub's up at four. What do you say?

— I say thank you.

— YIPPEEEEEEEEEEEEEEEEEEEEEEEEEEEEEEEE!
— YES YES YES YES!
— COMEONNNNNN!
— GET IN THERE YOU MAMA!

He tried to compose himself.

Deep breaths. Calm down.

They were told there was going to be a team meeting after work that day.

— YIPEEEEEEEEEEE!

Start again.

A compulsory meeting. Ooooh?

The staff had been speculating all day about what it could be, and when the Area Manager turned up, well, they all thought that's it: Game Over! The service is in for the chop. The council are withdrawing their funding. The newly elected BNP councillors would rather cut funding for the disabled and spend it on repatriating the borough's half-million Muslims.

No such thing.

The manageress was taking 'early retirement'.

See also: the old heave-ho.

— WAHOOOOOOOOOOOOOOOOOOOOOOO! YES!

She feigned some croc-croc-crocodile tears and the staff contrived a facsimile of boo-hoo-ness. The Area Manager went on to say that they weren't to worry – the manageress wouldn't be leaving until they'd appointed a new replacement. Adverts were in all the rags the following week and interviews would be held early in the New Year.

— Fucking YES!

— Someone that can do the job properly? PLEASE!

As they were leaving the Centre, the Area Manager took Antony's arm.

— Can I have a word in private, Antony?

He thought that's it: I'm in the shit now.

She said that a few people had been singing his praises and she would welcome his application for the position of Service Manager.

— Really?

— Really.

He smiled a toothy smile.

Then, looking all serious, she went,

— How's your counselling going?

It knocked the wind out of him.

— Fine.

— Good. I saw one for a few years. Nasty divorce, don't ask. She helped me turn my life around. You stick with it. You know you have my full support.

He wanted to whip out some mistletoe and give her a Christmas tonguing. She shook his hand and smiled, meaning: we've got rid of the f-f-f-fat cow at long last.

When he got back home, he rolled a J as long as his joy and poured a vodka as strong as his relief. And then he began.

IT'S IMPORTANT to supply slow and easy pressure to the neck. Transient hypoxia is what you're after; too much bilateral pressure to the carotid sinuses and you'll find yourself being taken away in a body bag.

You manipulate the tension on the neck and the resulting asphyxiation with the rope, the pulley system and your own body weight. Generally, this depends upon your system and weight and general fitness levels and whether or not you've been drinking or drugging to heighten the effect. But you have to be careful at the onset of orgasm, for split-second failure to release the mechanism, when you *literally* become weak at the knees, will result in suffocation and death.

You will die in three, not-so-easy stages:

1. Cyanosis. Carbon-dioxide retention will turn you a beautiful shade of blue. You'll be panicking. Your respiration will be fast, deep and erratic as you struggle to bre-bre-bre-breathe.
2. Vascular congestion and haemorrhage. Your breathing will be totally fucked. You'll be convulsing madly, struggling, kicking, fighting. Doing the hangman's dance.
3. Complete loss of consciousness. Dilated pupils, terminal vomiting. Your face will be covered in petechial haemorrhages; the epiglottis and subglottic spaces will be packed with blood; the pharynx and tonsils and tongue-root will be engorged.

It will take between two and five agonizing minutes for you to die.

HE SCREWED the hook-eyes in, tied the keys and passed the cordage and chain over the clothes pole, twisting, smiling, remembering his night up on Swarth Coum, remembering the end that became a beginning, how he hit the ground with something whispering down his veins. A voice in his head. A song in his skin.

IT WAS HIS LAST appointment with the psych for four weeks. The psych talked for ages about Antony's feelings towards the hands-off parenting of his childhood.

— Yes, it's lucky you had Eddie in your life, the psych said, but it's a parent's responsibility to mirror their children.

— What's 'mirror' mean?

— Approval and admiration. The child wants his parent to notice him, to praise him, to respect him. They should provide a role model.

Antony laughed.

— You have no debt to your parents, Antony. Yes, they let you down, and let you down terribly, but look at who you are *now*, at the person you've become. You're not a result of them.

The psych's face was full of compassion, but his words seemed dented, broken.

IT MANIFESTS ITSELF IN a nagging throb behind your ears, a sharp twinge along your sides, a spasm in the facial muscles that construct a malign sneer. It's the perennial cynicism that convinces you to finish masturbating, roll over, and sleep the day away. Formed in response to the prospect of spending yet another Christmas Day with someone else's family, someone else's loved ones, feeling at worst like an interloper, at best a spare part. It's the old Christmas spirit insisting you ignore texts and phone calls, draw the curtains, turn off the lights, get your favourite videos out, pour another drink, and don't even bother getting dressed.

Fuck Santa, it sings.

And you can stick consumerism and playing happy families up your arse.

But Antony did it: he dragged himself from the warm spot of his bed and stood before the window. Snow had yet to fall in the city, but the distant hills – they were dusted with the stuff.

JADE'S FOLKS' HOUSE was a spectacular Georgian four-storey beast with huge bay windows and a cupola at one end. The adjectival kind of house Antony had always dreamt of living in. Maybe in the next world.

Even the cab driver said 'nice' when he saw it.

Jade was her usual delish self in a pair of slouchy, wide-legged trousers and some nifty little boots and a shimmery V-neck that showed a tasty bit of cleavage. And you could see where she got her looks from: her mother was total yummy-mummy material. And when Antony was introduced to Eileen – no old school 'mum' and 'dad' monikers in their house – he shook her hand and went,

– You never told me you had a sister, Jade.

Eileen punched him softly on the shoulder and said,

– You'll do for me, creep. Come meet the others.

The living room was festooned with garlands of twinkling lights and had that Yule scent of pine, tinged with the gunpowder smell of pulled crackers. Antony noted a ravaged advent calendar; he noted baubles and tinsel, torn wrapping paper stuffed into black bin bags. A Christmas compilation was playing to about ten or twelve people scattered across the sofas and floor – a scene straight out of *The Waltons*. The only thing wrong with the picture was the depressed man standing within it who saw something not entirely normal.

A wagging golden retriever, Biscuit, gambolled over and nudged him with a cold wet nose, and Jade's dad, Pete, greeted Antony with a 'now then son', giving him a fierce manly handshake.

Antony pulled their presents from his bag: Pete's, a bottle of single malt anCnoc; Eileen's, a large bottle of Bombay Sapphire. They both made a lot of appreciative noise and he even got a peck on the cheek from Eileen.

Then John introduced him to Moon and signed an apology for his parents: Not to worry, they could escape to the village pub later on. Antony fingersigned back and John laughed; Antony was slurring his fingerspelling.

Jade took him to one side to give him his present: *Amnesiac* by Radiohead.

Was she trying to be funny?

EILEEN SERVED the food and they all got steadily pissed. There was some great banter between Eileen and Pete and everyone seemed relaxed and in high spirits. And then it hit him: this was why Jade was so mature and settled and at ease with herself: normal parents – what a complete oddity!

He pictured Kenneth at the unit, looking doleful in paper hat.

At one point during the afternoon, Eileen came and sat more or less on Antony's lap and started grilling him about his family and job and where he came from, et cetera.

He couldn't help it – he started undressing her with his eyes. Jade rescued him as he began to stutter, saying she'd give him a tour of the house.

As soon as they were upstairs she stuck a finger in his ribs.

— You're caned, aren't you?

Every time he blinked, he saw Eileen naked. A very pretty sight.

— Is it obvious?

— Just stop bloody smiling all the time. And stop flirting with Eileen.

She play-slapped his wrist.

— You got any with you?

He smiled again.

They walked the full length of the house and he counted five bedrooms, then she opened a door onto a narrow, winding staircase, and when they got near the top she stepped behind him and put her hands over his eyes.

— Trust me. Up a bit. That's it.

He heard a door creak. Felt an icy breeze.

— OK, open.

They were up in the cupola, lit by the same coloured fairy lights, he noted, that she had in her attic bedroom at her house 'up on the tops'. Below them, two deep valleys snaked out across snowy moors, and on the horizon, the urban orange light from Manchester and Oldham and Rochdale.

— Do you know how lucky you are?

— I know. Pete and Eileen are great. They're like my best friends. It's amazing to have these two wonderful people always on my side, cheering me on from the wings. They're kind and thoughtful and loving and affectionate and wise and . . .

As she gushed about her parents Antony found himself thinking that every child must know that one without the other is less, not more.

Jade was waving a hand in his face.

— Anybody there?

— Sorry. Here.

He pulled her present from his pocket. She peeled the wrapping from the box.

— Jesus, Ant. Is it real jade?

She fastened the clasp of the bracelet, her hands shaking slightly.

— You can tell, he said, by touching the stones. By how cold they are.

— Just like me?

He noticed how she'd stare at him before speaking. She'd

blink a few times, her lips opened as she paused, her small nose flaring slightly. And what made her so truly adorable was the fact that she wasn't even aware how adorable she was. Her eyes unbuttoned him. Uncertain what to say next, he licked his lips, nodded once and went,

— Go on.

— You're such a nice guy, Ant.

— I don't feel like a nice guy. I feel dead inside.

— But I don't see you like that. Only you see yourself like that.

He shrugged.

— You're caring. Thoughtful. Sensitive.

— I'm a mess.

— We're all a mess. We're all struggling.

He could hear his heart beat.

— None of us know how to live our lives.

He watched her bracelet slide the length of her forearm.

— Is it too big? I can have it altered.

—It's perfect, Ant.

She opened her arms and they held each other tightly.

Her voice into his jumper,

— Let's not fall out ever again, eh.

They held each other for a while, listening to the sleepy sound of wind whistling through the cupola. She looked up at him, tilting her head slowly, and he felt her soft open lips on his. The heat of her breath in his mouth. But their teeth clashed and she pulled away quickly.

— What?

John and Moon appeared. The four of them stood silently as the heat of a pheromone-flush prickled Antony's cheeks.

John signed: So who has the weed?

Antony's eyes, Jade's eyes – the cupola was bright with sparks.

THEY MADE their way along narrow, country-dark lanes to the village pub. Antony sat beside John for most of the night, but he couldn't concentrate on John's frenetic hands – his mouth tingled, his eyes kept flashing over at Jade's. Smirks, grins, beams, flashes. Obvious doesn't even begin to describe it.

The four of them got back some time after midnight to find all the guests had left. Pete, halfway through his bottle of anCnoc, was watching *Father Ted* on his new DVD player, chuckling away to himself.

Antony popped his M and that was the last thing he could remember; waking up beside Jade, he freaked: he thought, just for a painful nanosecond, that it was Rebecca, and was thankful he still had his underpants on.

Jade nudged him sleepily; he held her until she nodded back off.

He dressed quietly and considered leaving a note on the pillow next to her.

A solitary, emotive X.

Then he saw himself do it: he took a pair of knickers from her bedroom floor and stuffed them into his coat pocket.

THE CAB DRIVER SAID he was on his way back from Bradford and he'd be there in ten.

Antony looked up at the house, thinking about the sleeping family inside, thinking he might like a family of his own one day. He'd be a Pete and Jade would be an Eileen, they'd even have a golden retriever called Biscuit and a deaf raver son and a daughter who wouldn't know what to do with her life.

But the warm fluffy picture dissolved as soon as he got home:

A pair of slutty six-inch heels on the floor.
The montage of women's faces on one wall.
The closet door open, a length of cordage hanging from the clothes pole.
A crumpled dress on the back of a chair.

He climbed onto the bed and buried his face in
    Rebecca's T-shirt.
His tear valves burst their banks. A hot wetness slicked
    his face.
Inside: he grasped around.
He felt the presence of a hand in his.

She was here again.

But the sudden chill of her absence, a falling feeling that
made him gasp,
    — WAIT!

THEY'RE MY BEST FRIENDS. Mirroring. Approval. Admiration. He could say the words but they held nothing. He knew this was what other people had, that this was normal; a childhood being noticed, respected. There were times, way back, a handful of moments when he remembered it being just the two of them. Before Lou. Before the permanent glass in his mother's hand. A time when laughter and light filled the house.

But it hurt to remember.

Like he was watching another life.

SMUG FAT-FUCK BOUNCERS stood in heated doorways watching the season slice the huddled queue with its wintry knife. Luckily John had stuck the three of them on the guest list and so when Jade and Moon eventually turned up the three of them got to jump. The club was better than Antony expected, with different deejays and veejays in about six different rooms. The place stank of gange and Red Bull and dry ice, and there were an inordinate amount of crusties and chavvy rave-heads sitting on top of the bass bins, blissed-out and swaying.

They managed to find a good spot in the room where John was deejaying and began caning the drugs. Twenty minutes later, Jade was sat on his lap, burying her face in his neck and sighing hotly,

— Coming up?

— Like a bastard.

They stroked each other's fingers, relaying secret messages.

— Thank you, she said. For sending Eileen the flowers. She was proper made up.

— It's probably the only Christmas Day I've ever enjoyed.

He squeezed her tightly.

— Your parents are tops, he said.

Meaning maybe with you I could be normal.

They held each other's gaze in a prolonged and nuanced mind-read. They kissed long and deep and he felt something come undone, let go inside. Their brains began to soar and they had to dance. Bodies, limbs, minds entwined, smiling face to smiling face, they buckled themselves in for twists and turns, for the feigned E drop-offs.

HE NIPPED into an empty cubicle and stood for ages, eyes watering as he strained. A sign above the cistern read: KEEP DEPRESSED. It made him giggle. He huffed and pushed for another minute, but thought fuck it; his urethra was swollen. Dirty pills.

He filled his water bottle up and wandered back out into the pounding amphetamine beat and found himself in a room playing horrendously stark speed garage. He stood and watched bug-eyed teenaged boys twitching spastically in the sweat-foggy air, a multitude of wall-mounted cine-projectors throwing psychedelic images over their starved, cut-tone bodies. And the pretty little clotheshorses up on the podiums, self-satisfied in their strappy little dresses and micro-skirts, their Scary Spice hairdos and old-skool trainers. Things change, he thought. Things become less subtle.

He realized his eyeballs were vibrating.

He wandered for a while until he saw a face he recognized: Bone Head from Cheaper Sounds. Antony went up to him and, quite inappropriately, gave him a tight hug.

Then Antony saw the rest of the employees.

And then he saw Rebecca.

HE RAN AFTER HER and grabbed her arm, adrenalin screaming through his blood.

She stopped and looked at her feet.

— Can we talk?

She folded her arms, flooding his heart with love.

— Just for a minute, he said. Please. There's something I
need to tell you.

All the stupid things he'd done, all the trouble he'd caused
– it was there in her eyes, striking his heart like hammers.

That hard glitter. That visual silence.

— I'm not going to let you fuck up my night, Ant. Say what
you want to say and fuck off. Or better still, leave the fucking
club.

He bumped into her in a club and this is what she said:
leave.

She nodded at someone behind him. Bone Head. He
looked at Antony, looked at Rebecca, then shrugged and
walked away.

She seemed to say: Just spit it out.

— I'm sorry, he said.

— You're fucking joking, right?

— I'm sorry for everything.

— And that's supposed to make it better?

— I'm seeing a therapist, he said.

127

She laughed. Snarky. Snide. That citric smile.

— I admit, he said. I was depressed.

The way she let her hair cover her eyes, hiding her thoughts.

— I know you'll never take me back. I know I've ruined it for ever. But I just want you to know that it wasn't your fault.

Incredulous.

— It was me, he said. I ruined it. I lied to you. I was just scared of losing you. And I was right, wasn't I?

You could see the memory unfold in her eyes. She was even more beautiful than he remembered. She moved away but he ran after her and grabbed her arm. She turned and slapped his face in a single, fluid movement.

— Fuck off, you FREAK!

— Doesn't what we had *mean* anything?

— Does it fuck.

Looking at him with such repulsion, such indignation, Antony's entire brain chemistry transformed. His adrenal gland vomited, forcing his hippocampus to hallucinate a triptych of unwanted memories:

1. The thick mucus sound of her sobbing as she ran out of the flat the last time;
2. The warm chaos of fucking, her gasp-muttered words, their bodies melting into hard, bucking orgasm;
3. The night in Wales when their eyes locked as they both said yes simultaneously. Yes, let's make a go of it. Yes.

A tap on his shoulder.

Jade.

— What's going on?

Idiotically, he smiled. Idiotically, he said,

— Jade, this is Rebecca. Rebecca, this is Jade.

And he was, quite suddenly, alone.

The music stopped. The clubbers kept dancing.
Fake bells began to chime.

They're shouting, Ten.
They're shouting, Nine.
They're shouting, Eight.

HE FOUND HIMSELF reading it again – the last email Rebecca
sent him, five months before.

```
SUBJECT: Re: Please talk to me
----------------------------------------------
Drop dead. Get it through your THICK fucking
skull that it's OVER. Please stop phoning me
and harassing me or I mean it, I'll go to the
fucking police.
You know, I always thought it was my fault.
That I was doing something wrong. I've felt
like that for over a year now and you knew and
said NOTHING. I never want to see you again as
long as I live.
Face it, I can never make you happy. I can never
give you what you really want. And I don't want
to be in anyone's fucking closet.
I was getting fucking sick and tired of you
anyway. You've damaged any future we had
together.
Stop mailing. Let go. It's over.
```

HE WATCHED THE BLADE passing over the pale, soft under-side of his forearm, depressing blue veins, willing himself to slice deeper, deeper. Lying on his kitchen floor in a pool of blood? Waiting for hours to slip into an icy unconsciousness? No. He wanted guests sat around a hospital bed. He wanted concerned psychs tapping pens between their teeth, listening intently. Just someone, anyone, to notice.

Tell me about the first time you met your father.

He couldn't even break the skin.

Subject: Please talk to me
>
>This doesn't have to be the end Rebecca. It
>really doesn't. We can still make a go of
>things. We can still talk through this.
>Our love is too important to throw away. I'll
>change. Why did you say you'd fucking marry me
>if you knew you didn't love me?
>Just fucking TALK TO ME!
>
>Please. I will always, always love you.
>A

THE COME-DOWN was oppressive. His serotonin had been gang-raped, his alpha$_2$ receptors were a whore's spread legs and his 5HT$_2$ and $_3$ receptors were a 'Girlfriend in a Coma'. He wept at the weather forecast. He wept as Harold played his tuba on *Neighbours*. He wanted to be locked away, sectioned.

There'll be a time in the future when you'll need to see her.

He stared at the drawings of Rebecca on the walls and wanted to disappear.

He knew it'd pass – it was just a couple of days of come-down blues.

But it was a fucking killer.

My Documents. My Music. Rebecca.

Six audio files:

1. 'Oh'
2. 'Aaagh'
3. 'Yes'
4. 'Oh Antony'
5. 'Don't hurt me'
6. 'Please'

He used to hide his Dictaphone on the bedside table and record him and Rebecca fucking, and then he'd edit them down on Media Player – he'd edit the sections where he could hear her gasping. It became his wanking soundtrack.

5. 'Don't hurt me' was his favourite.

Who do you punish, Antony?

Like she's choking to death.

He remembered how he'd wake in the middle of the night, bladder bursting, his cock so hard it hurt, the twine wrapped tightly around his wrist, securing him to the bed.

He'd hold on for as long as he could, but then he'd have to let it go. The release, the scratchy burn of piss.

Because he walked in his sleep.

Because he fell down stairs.

Because he wandered out.

So Mother tied him to the bed at night, until the school complained about the marks. Until they mentioned Social Services. But that was Val's shame, not hers, and so released him into the night. But it was too late:

Erection = pain = breathlessness = release = shame.

His hard drive was formatted.

HE ASKED REBECCA if he could wear her knickers while they made love, just around an ankle. No way. He told her he wanted her to call him names. It's embarrassing. So he asked her to play dead, to pose like a Dumas painting. Hold your breath. Don't move. So she'd lie there, motionless, watching him through the blur of her lashes. Once, he asked her to choke him, to strangle him while they made love. Her face said I don't know you. So he positioned her thumbs over the carotid and asked her to press. I'm scared. He found a scarf and asked her to pull it tight, just when he was about to come.

Fuck you.

He wanted a way out, an accomplice, someone to help him escape the endless keep going, the more more more of it, trying to embellish every single sensory stimulation. So come on, keep going keep going, choke me, strangle me, choke choke choke, kill kill kill, yes FUCKING KILL ME because danger is pleasure and pleasure is . . .

DELETE DELETE DELETE DELETE DELETE DELETE
DELETE DELETE DELETE DELETE DELETE DELETE
DELETE DELETE DELETE DELETE DELETE DELETE
DELETE DELETE DELETE DELETE DELETE DELETE
DELETE DELETE DELETE DELETE DELETE DELETE
DELETE DELETE DELETE DELETE DELETE DELETE
DELETE DELETE DELETE DELETE DELETE DELETE
DELETE DELETE DELETE DELETE DELETE DELETE
DELETE DELETE DELETE DELETE DELETE DELETE
DELETE DELETE DELETE DELETE DELETE DELETE
DELETE DELETE DELETE DELETE DELETE DELETE
DELETE DELETE DELETE DELETE DELETE DELETE
DELETE DELETE DELETE DELETE DELETE DELETE
DELETE DELETE DELETE DELETE DELETE DELETE
DELETE DELETE DELETE DELETE DELETE DELETE
DELETE DELETE DELETE DELETE DELETE DELETE
DELETE DELETE DELETE DELETE DELETE DELETE
DELETE DELETE DELETE DELETE DELETE DELETE
DELETE DELETE DELETE DELETE DELETE DELETE
DELETE DELETE DELETE DELETE DELETE DELETE
DELETE DELETE DELETE DELETE DELETE DELETE
DELETE DELETE DELETE DELETE DELETE DELETE
DELETE DELETE DELETE DELETE DELETE DELETE
DELETE DELETE DELETE DELETE DELETE DELETE

THE INVISIBLE PATH THAT led from his bedroom, down the stairs and out across the backfields. Stepping through gorse and heather in his jarmies, hands before him, eyes closed into the night. Wandering woods, fingers grasping, he'd see himself stepping out of his skin, following an invisible path into the night as moor-wind raked his hair. He'd smell the body of another as the noisy night shivered: foxes jabbering on their slinking night-prowl; rabbits gripped in stone-hard yellow talons, squealing overhead; inward-bound bats with their shrill chirrups, flinging themselves around moorland bluffs. And the twit-twooing of ghost-white, apple-faced *Tyto alba*, testing the air in the echoing woodland.

Nature, waiting for the Blue Hour.

He'd raise his arms.

Feel someone touching his dreams.

V

JADE'S VOICE had a blur to it. A kind of fatigue.

— I'm sorry, he said.

— It's fine.

— I just bumped into her.

— Whatever.

— I had no idea she was going to be there.

— Course.

— I don't understand why you're so upset.

— You wouldn't.

— She means *nothing* to me any more. I know that now.

— Now?

— . . .

— I stood and watched you, Ant. I know what I saw.

— . . .

— Listen, a guy in the village.

— What?

— He's asked me out.

— Oh really?

— Yeah.

— Why you telling me?

— Thought you'd like to know.

— Why don't you?

— What?

— Go out for a date.

— . . .

— With 'The Guy From The Village'.

— . . .

— Why don't you say yes?

— I'll do that.

— Yeah, you *do* that.

WHAT JADE didn't hear that afternoon was the sound of Antony's heart violating itself as he realized he was totally, and utterly, in love with her.

HE PRESSED the number for the Centre.

— I've got a stomach bug. I don't think I'll make it in today.

Trudy, for some reason, seemed very disappointed.

He got the bus to Lizzie's. There was a light on inside. He knocked three times before a shower-wet, disgruntled Sarah appeared.

— What do you want?

— I need to talk.

She left the door open and clomped up the stairs.

Antony sat at the kitchen table and listened to the hum of hairdryer and slam of doors. Sat in that room again, he realized how much he missed his outreach sessions.

Kenneth's wit. His vigour. His riotous foul-mouth.

Sarah came back down and placed an envelope in front of him.

— What's this?

— Open it.

Inside the envelope was a file; inside the file were Kenneth's medical case notes from Manchester Memorial Hospital. Antony was sure he'd seen them before, but then he checked the date: November 26th 1995.

He read, still not sure what he was meant to be looking for. Sarah sat beside him.

— So?

Antony shrugged.

She tutted and snatched the file. She pointed to an acronym: A.V.E.

— You know what that means?

His eyes searched the ceiling. He said slowly,

— Acute viral encephalitis? So?

She pointed again.

— And that?

The letters: HSV-2.

He shrugged.

— Look, she said. 'Prodromal symptoms including genital lesions'.

— But that doesn't . . .

— Dad was having an affair.

Antony searched her eyes.

— You don't like me, do you, she said. You think I'm horrible to Dad?

— It's really none of my.

— No, that's the whole point. We appreciate everything you've done for him, but to be honest, he's better off where he is. And yes, Mum *is* seeing someone else.

— I'm happy for her.

Sarah's face trembled.

— He went and cheated on Mum with some *slag* from the congregation and *we* had to suffer the consequences. Now fuck off out of our lives. And *stay* out.

ANTONY WANDERED along Manchester's streets feeling like a Lowry figure – so tiny, so insect-like. He checked his watch: the pubs wouldn't open for another hour. He found a corner shop and bought six Stella for a fiver and sat on a bench beside the road and started on his first can. He retched at the taste, but forced it down his neck, wiping his mouth with the back of his hand and belching with a flourish.

His thoughts turned to Jade. Her pureness, truthfulness, gorgeousness. And she was with someone else. Served him right for being such a knob. He felt locked onto that bench, as locked as his mind was on finishing those six cans and then phoning her to tell her he was sorry, that he loved her, and that Rebecca was nothing but a fucking bitch and he was better off without her.

Cars and lorries sped past a young, well-dressed man getting drunk on a bench at 10:00 a.m. on a Monday morning. Once begun, this is how it starts. He would stay out of everyone's business. He would fuck off out of everyone's lives. He finished the can and opened another, nodding to himself as a raw, wind-blown rain started to pour in diagonal sheets. He tied his hair back and realized he didn't even own an umbrella. He looked up into the dismal pall of the north-western skies for an explanation that never came.

AN HOUR LATER he was making his way to the tram stop when his trousers buzzed him.

— Hi, Antony, how you doing?

The Area Manager. He tried not to slur,

— You know, stomach flu, I think. Just off to the doc's.

— Did you know today's the deadline for internal applications?

— I did. Aye.

— But we haven't received yours yet.

— No. I know.

— Oh.

He couldn't focus properly. He blinked and saw Eddie's comb-over.

— Do you not intend to apply, Antony?

Blinked and saw Derek's man-boobs.

— No. I don't.

Blinked again and saw a closed-caption balloon in his head: FUCK YOU.

— That's a real shame.

— Is it?

— You didn't hear this from me, but you stand a very good chance.

— But nothing will change.

— I'm sorry?

— Nothing will ever change.

— Oh.

— You can't polish a turd.

— Sorry?

— Thank for your encouragement.

— Oh. Right. Goodbye, then. I . . .

He hung up and climbed onto the tram and tried to stay awake. He went to OUTBOX on his mobile and re-read the last message he sent to her:

```
hi j just wanna say hello
hope yr ok? b good 2 spk
soon A x
```

Resting his head against the cool glass, watching life's blur, he travelled back in time. He was in Warsaw, stepping into his three layers of clothes and peering out the window, waiting for the tram to pull into the stop before he joined the pack of fur coats rushing from the forest of tower blocks. They'd huddle together, all a-shiver, scraping ice off the inside of the windows to see their stops.

He walked slowly up Woodlands Road, stopping outside the Mosque to look back at the bleak skyline of Saddleworth interrupted by the grey tower blocks of Oldham. Then he bought a kebab from the Burning Balti and sat in the park opposite his flat, eating ravenously, dripping sauce onto his shoes.

He wanted more. More junk, more beer, more nicotine.

The thought of returning to the flat, of his own company. Fuck that.

HE WOKE UP BREATHLESS on the floor, heart pounding. He rolled a rollie and opened the window. The cloying stench of curry made him gip.

Cheetham Hill at dawn. Place of bedsits and takeaways, snide shops selling brand-name knock-offs, place of Jewish and Asian delis, pound shops and Bollywood Video stores. He looked at those streets and pictured all the dog shite and needles, all the nettles and johnnies and broken bottles. He saw razor ribbons snaking atop the backyard walls that seemed to fill the freakishly treeless city.

He was still fully clothed. Still had his shoes on. His sleeve smelled of vomit.

When he blinked, he saw blue-green bottles of beer against the green baize of a pool table, and he remembered sitting alone in a pub, sneering at some monkey-walking, hoody teenagers, thinking: their music makes me ill, their tone of voice, their stupid fashions and hairstyles. Then he saw the image of the canal path as he wended his way home, the motionless Rochdale Canal so black and slab-like in the moonlight.

He couldn't even remember if he made it to his dealer's or not.

He selected Jade's number on his mobile, and as it purred he imagined her clambering from her bed, a ghost in her sheer blue nightgown.

Her thin sleepy voice,
— Hello?
He went into the bathroom and hurled his guts into the toilet bowl.

HE LEANED OVER and put his ear to the receiver. He could hear Jade breathing on the other end. He went into the kitchen, put some bread into the toaster and flicked the kettle on. He leaned against the washing machine where he could see the receiver resting on the arm of the settee.

He wondered how long it would be before she hung up.

THE SURPRISE OF SNOW. It had settled in the city throughout the night and lay thick on rooftops, throughout the streets, big wet snowflakes falling slantwise, pearling his windows. He'd experienced snow. Extreme snow. Poland marked the end of his three lost years in black-and-white, and he arrived just in time for the worst winter in twenty-five years. At minus 30° your breath crackles as it leaves your mouth. The moisture on your eyes begins to stick. Jewellery burns your skin. The air congeals inside your nasal cavity. Pipes explode in the street. Joints throb and skin blisters. And as life turned an icy monotone, the woman in the mirror was still there. But by the end of April he could smell the temperature rise – a winter's worth of dog turds, millions of them curled and frozen into the ice, began to melt, and Antony found himself down by the river Wisła every night just to get some air. He watched huge blocks of ice, three storeys high, floating downstream, and on the very last day of winter he saw a dog frozen onto the top of an ice block – he could see the shocking pink of its tongue. It was the first colour he'd seen for months.

PANOPTICAL STRANGEWAYS. He could just make out the rooftops of the central hall last night, and imagined the prisoners inside, watching the flakes fall beyond the barred windows, thinking about how much they missed hearing the sound of their children in the morning. They might see them in the occasional monthly visit – those ill-at-ease moments of faux-smiles and tongue-tied silences – but Antony knew there'd be little laughter involved. Jack's hard, thin mattress. The scratches on the wall. The hish of Jack's feet walking circuitous circles of eight.

It was Antony's eleventh birthday. He'd been awake for over an hour, breathing warmth into his hands, listening to the house click and sigh.

His mother's voice on the landing,

— Shift your arse.

He shivered, staring at his naked reflection in the mirror. Smudge of eyes. Dilute-milk, chiffon skin. Pebble joints. Tight walnut scrotum, squab-bald cock, trumpet foreskin. Acky. Death warmed up.

He wanted, one day, to see something else.

There was a noise like gunshots outside. He rubbed a porthole through the condensation. Eddie's old banger, back-firing down the street.

He dressed quickly and ran from the house without a word.

The car reeked of polish and an eggy smell came from the heater.

— So how do you feel? You nervous?

His insides were loose.

— No.

Eddie scraped the car into gear but they didn't move.

Antony looked at the house. The dark shape of his mother at the window.

He didn't know where Lou was. Didn't care.

— It'll be a grand day. You'll remember this for the rest of your life, son.

— Let's go, Eds.

— Hang on.

Eddie held out a tie. It was purple and had a big metal clip on the back.

— But I'll look like a knob.

— Do up your top button. Howay.

His mother's eyes, watching.

AS THEY HIT the dual carriageway, Antony could see the gypsy caravans and the industrial estate over to his left. The ice-cream factory where his mother worked, perched in the rocks and couch grass, the smashed cement and nettles, tall metallic chimneys sprouting out of it all, billowing sweet-smelling white crap.

Beyond it all: the fells and summits of Swarth Coum.

He tried to slow his mind, watching the scenery film-flickering by, the hillsides decorated with tall green pine trees looming large against the terracotta morning.

Today was the day and he wondered how he'd got here.

Finally, ninety minutes from the hills, the city loomed frantically on the skyline.

THE ORANGE BRICKS of the prison walls were rain-splotched purple. Barbed wire snaked atop the high perimeter fence. High on one wall, a clock hung. The further in he went, the more he felt trapped. Within the gates the light seemed to change. Light, air and space, riven by metal against metal. The gates locked crashing behind them as they moved deeper.

— Turn your pockets into the tray and walk through the machine.

He was embarrassed by the photos: Mother in the left side, Jack in the right.

More gates. Clunking. Echoing. Blank-faced screws everywhere. The place smelled of men. The low mutter of their voices.

They entered a room full of tables. Screws stood sentry in each corner, hands behind their backs, pigeon-chests stuck out. All of these men – it terrified him. He recognized that look in their eyes: they thought he was scum.

A booming voice,

– Ellis. J.E.9.5.6.0.

Antony turned to Eddie; Eddie smiled.

Jack. Father. Dad. A giant of a man in an orange bib.

An off-white smile beneath a thick bracket of black moustache.

So this is him.

This is what you look like.

HE WONDERED HOW ILL she really was. Ill with the drink, that's what Jack said. And Lou had gone. He found it hard to imagine: his mother alone.

He checked his mobile and looked at the last message from Jack. Her address and phone number in Cornwall. He jotted it down on a piece of paper and chose erase all.

WHENEVER LOU LEFT, his mother would sit in the bathtub listening to Motown all night, her voice rattling like a chainsaw. They were songs of the darkest love. Sombre. Dismal. It sounded so painful being grown up. 'Seven Rooms of Gloom'. 'You Keep Me Hanging On'. 'Standing in the Shadow of Love'. 'I'm Losing You'. 'Remember Me'. 'Love is Here and Now You're Gone'. The Motown sound meant home to him.

HE EXPECTED A LECTURE about his 'lack of commitment'; he expected to be served a final written warning. But no one said a thing when he turned up that Friday. The manageress had become a ghost.

He was telling the pysch about New Year's Eve, about seeing Rebecca, and Jade's reaction.

— Do you think, the psych asked, that you might be a little bit too demanding? Maybe too critical of others?

Antony shrugged and rubbed his hands, thinking I thought you were on my side. He realized the psych was observing his movements, his body language. Antony felt his muscles tauten.

— Have you felt any resentment from others? Recently, I mean.

— Definitely, Antony said. *Yes*.

You're getting it now.

— OK. And have you ever considered the idea that maybe you create certain problems for yourself? That perhaps you generate these kinds of conflicts?

After a while of staring out the window, Antony changed his posture in a way he hoped belied his anger.

— How is your drinking and drug-taking at the moment?

— I'm cutting down.

— Are you getting any exercise?

Antony frowned.

— It'll make you feel better, the psych said. Physically and mentally.

— Aren't endorphins or peptides just natural opiates?

The psych smiled wearily: don't be a clever-dick.

— I'll check out the local gym, he said.

THAT NIGHT, Antony had a bubble bath and then changed into the floral print dress that he'd bought from a charity shop. He stood, deliciously horny in front of the mirror, the sight its usual turn-on, but realized how he desperately needed to update his wardrobe.

I look like Freddy Mercury in the 'I Want To Break Free' video.

I resemble some saddo housewife circa 1984.

There was still no response from Jade.

Surely she'd want to know why he'd called but hadn't spoken.

He pictured her fucking The Guy From The Village. He saw a young George Clooney making her gasp and squeal with wide-mouthed pleasure to the rapid, metrical bang of a headboard.

So it was to be another Friday night in on his own, sat on his couch in a pretty dress with a *Friends* double-bill, a bottle of Jacobs Creek, and succession of fat Js for company.

I'm an advertiser's wet dream.

HE WASN'T SURE whether to believe Sarah about Kenneth being unfaithful, but she was right on one score: Lizzie had a new man. Antony got to the unit an hour earlier that Saturday and saw a figure in her parked car. He walked past as casually as he could: a man inside, fiddling with the stereo. So average. So middle-aged. So forgettable.

Kenneth was sat in the back garden, smoking. It was blustery. He looked cold.

— You all right, Kenneth?

Antony waited for him to suck his cigarette down and flick it away.

— Has Lizzie been?

— Yeah, Antony said. She just left.

— Oh right. Good.

— Has Sarah been to see you?

— Who?

— Fancy a game of *Shit Scrabble Fuck*?

Kenneth stood up and waved a fist in Antony's face.

— Prepare yourself for a good fucking thrashing.

Later, they went up to his room and Antony found the walls were covered with scraps of paper: words, sentences, pictures, arrows, maps in Kenneth's hand. On one piece of paper the word: HOME?

Kenneth started padding his hands around the walls. He turned to Antony.

— Toilet. Right. End of corridor. Right. Watch me.

Antony noticed the background noise of the unit for the first time, the faint pad of Kenneth's footfalls along the carpeted hallway, swing doors sighing in soft declension. Such sleepy sounds.

He went over to Kenneth's chest of drawers and removed the backing from the picture frame. On the back of the baby photo, a date: January 5th 1990.

He replaced the backing and sat down on the bed.

Above Kenneth's headboard, the words: DREAM OF MAKING.

Kenneth appeared.

— The white coats? Antony asked.

— Who?

— The doctors, Kenneth. Why wouldn't they let you in to see her?

He sat on the bed and took Antony's hand.

— Has Lizzie been?

— Yes. She came this morning, mate.

Kenneth went to the wall and pulled a piece of paper off and handed it to Antony. On it, he'd written: ANTONY CUNTING DOBSON.

— Keep it, Kenneth said. In case you forget you're a cunt!

Kenneth laughed maniacally, and then, quite sternly, asked Antony to go.

HE DIDN'T DEMAND anything from anyone. He was only critical of those who deserved it. The thought that he was like her, that he was recreating the drunken turmoil that span between her and Lou, recreating those hard moments, trapped in their echoes – he felt the cracks of himself.

BEEFCAKES GRUNTING like animals to trashy R'n'B, and the guy showing him around the place was buff and camp as Christmas. So this was it: working out. After the mind-numbing demonstration, Antony pumped iron for maybe five whole minutes and was bored shitless. Mostly, he sat and watched the others: mainly miserable-looking young women who looked like they needed a good feed. They strained, they paused, they heaved, they sweated. Stair climbers, free weights, rowing machines, elliptical trainers. Instruments of torture. Ageing. Gravity. Love handles. Burning themselves away. The most exciting moment was witnessing some old woman wearing headphones who kept farting weedily, unawares, on a step machine. Antony felt stupid and skinny and weak and so he left, promising himself never to grace such a theatre of freaks ever again.

In the dream, he saw his mother in the living room with the TV switched off, smoking, the permanent glass in her hand. He felt the invisible line that attached them both – he felt it wrapped around his heart, tightening. He couldn't remember the last time he'd heard her laugh.

SPARKLE
SUNSHINE GRINNING
POWERFUL
GLITTERING EXCITING

CHEEKY

JOYFUL

EXUBERANT SENSUOUS

HARMONY YOU!

LYING IN BED FOR the past hour, wondering how Jade would react to her Valentine's card and the cheese-on-toast poem inside. He'd surfed the Net for love poems, but most were a load of adjectival wank about Lovely Roses or Drunken Kisses or Haths and Hath-Nots. He remembered Jade saying she liked Ted Hughes, but all of his poems seemed to be about clarty-arsed sheep. Then he found one by an American poet – something about the world beating like a slackened drum when she wasn't around.

He regretted it as soon as he posted it.

So, what delights awaited him that day?

Well, 10:00 a.m. saw the first of the interviews for the Service Manager's post. Four short-listed interviewees and Antony was on the Spaz Panel; it was a way of putting the candidates on the spot, to see whether they could handle Derek's churlish ramblings and Lerch's shambling misery.

At least it meant he'd miss Smoke Club that afternoon.

He took some toilet roll from his bedside table and wiped his wrist, listening to 'This Charming Man' belting out, and then he stood in front of the bathroom mirror grinning at himself, reciting the list of lipsticked words, trying to invoke their meaning.

He'd started rubbing some of them off; scared their powers of persuasion were losing their impact.

THE SHORTLISTEES looked completely out of their depth. First, Antony nodded to Lerch and observed the candidate while Lerch grunted and gasped, his arm juddering slowly closer to the Big Mac Button switch. Eventually, he managed to hit it, activating the recorded message: Antony's distorted voice saying,

— What are your feelings on disabilism?

And all the shortlistees replied,

— What's disabilism?

Antony fielded the question to Derek.

— Treating. Us. Like. Inferior. Beings.

Then they asked the candidates about managing volunteers, fundraising, the Disability Discrimination Act and their views on advocacy and Independent Living.

They had a staff meeting after work to discuss the top two, and there was much discussion over whether they could 'mould' the candidate. They decided to go with the guy with the sad spectacles. They nicknamed him 'Spooner' because he kept getting his words muddled up.

He'd fit right in.

Still no response from Jade.

LATE AT NIGHT, he watched cars passing in the street below. He wondered about the passengers inside and where the road would take them tonight. He imagined it was twenty years ago and that it was his mother travelling home from the factory. He saw her pulling into the drive. Saw her sitting in the dark, listening to the engine click. Mouth open, eyes screwed tight, as Lou waited for her inside. She saw Lou's pockmarked face. Lou's tattooed fist in her mind, opening, closing. It was the only time she ever felt alive.

THE PSYCH MADE a long-fingered steeple with his hands and the opening strains of 'Eleanor Rigby' filled Antony's head. The psych nodded,

— Go on.

Antony worried about the Dictaphone in his breast pocket – worried the psych would see it or that he might accidentally knock it and press rewind and then play and their recorded, metallic-sounding voices would fill the room. But after a while he simply forgot it was there.

— I've been thinking a lot about the sessions, Antony said. And I've been thinking a lot about what went on in my childhood. And I feel like I've reached a barrier. That I can talk and talk but there's nothing I can really connect with.

No response was always a response, a kind of invitation.

— I don't know whether it's because that time was so . . . I don't know. There's part of me now that feels a real need to connect with what happened. Maybe I need something more dynamic than just sitting here talking, because I feel talking's only going to get me so far. Does that make any sense?

— Can you say a bit more about that?

— I feel that I'm talking around it. It's always worried me that I have these memories but there's nothing connecting them. I can't really connect with the *emotions* from that time.

I mean, it's like I can't remember what it was actually like to *be* a child. Maybe I'm thinking about it too much?

— I'm hearing you can remember what happened but not what you felt?

Antony knew he'd reached a brick wall, another impasse, and that he didn't want to reveal what, or who, was at the other side.

— I want to know if there's another type of therapy I could try? Another approach? Something more dynamic? Maybe hypnotherapy? I don't know. Something to help me access these memories, help string them together properly. Make them linear.

— And if you could make them linear, how would things be different? How would *life* be different?

— Because I feel what happened *then* is still steering my life *now*, especially my relationships.

— Are you talking about Rebecca? Jade?

— I do things and say things. I act in ways I don't understand.

No response.

— I need to understand why I keep doing this, why I find it hard to connect with people, why I keep pushing people away, why I keep making myself so fucking unlovable.

No response.

— I fucked up Rebecca's . . . I just don't . . .

No response.

— I was a shouter. A slammer. A walker-out-of-rooms.

No response.

— Maybe a chronology would reveal things about how I treat people *now*?

They repositioned themselves in the chairs. Antony stared at the tree pitching slowly in the wind outside. Eventually the psych cleared his throat.

— So you're concerned about your relationships *now*, and how you think remembering past emotions will help with that.

That might be true, but we know that memory is a funny thing. It's a reconstructive process. It isn't like reaching into an album and finding an old photograph. There are a lot of things that are difficult to reconstruct after a period of time, and if you manage to reconstruct them, then you may actually distort your memories. So what I think you're asking for is something that therapy doesn't necessarily deliver safely. You're right of course, if you talk about something a lot, it doesn't have the same emotional resonance. You desensitize it. But in a way a lot of that is good. And I'm not sure that . . .

The psych started scratching his neck vigorously.

A tickle of tears built in Antony's eyes. He looked over his shoulder.

It felt like somebody else was in the room.

The psych looked at the clock and brought his hands together with a clap.

Antony heard himself say it,

— Sometimes I dress in women's clothes.

The psych's face was unchanging.

— Sometimes I do weird things. Sexual things.

Antony put his hands to his throat.

The psych went,

— Go on.

But Antony barged out of there. He ran from the room and out of the clinic. The cold was straight into him as he dashed to the end of the street, feeling like he had a big neon sign attached to his head, flashing:

P-E-R-V-E-R-T
P-E-R-V-E-R-T
P-E-R-V-E-R-T

IT WAS ALL GOING wrong. He still felt like that boy trapped in that house, tied to his bed. Focus on the *now*. Focus. But it was all going tits-up. Why had he said it, confessed it? The breath play. He hadn't felt the need for weeks. He should've kept his mouth shut. The psych left a message on his mobile, saying if you need to talk before Friday I'll fit you in. Otherwise, I'll see you on Friday as per. But he didn't want to go. Maybe there'd be the police there. Maybe they'd lock him up – sectioned, for his own good. Maybe that's what he'd wanted all along. Someone to notice. Maybe that's why he blabbed? But he felt as if he'd really fucked up. It was ruining his life. All of this remembering. Sometimes, temporarily, he did forget. Drugs, drink, glue, ropes. But he'd never forget for long. And so he wanted to make himself anew. Rid himself of a self wrought by others. Start again. Afresh.

HE EVENTUALLY got a text from Jade.

b good 2 speak soon x

He couldn't help it, he read the subtext: I've been comparing you to The Guy From The Village, and, so far, he keeps coming out on top.

REBECCA WAS IN THE shower singing that Everything But The Girl tune, when he noticed her underwear on the bed and suddenly he was taking his clothes off and slipping her knickers on, but they were too tight so he put his arms through the straps of her bra and looked at himself in the mirror, pumping to the hish of the shower water, it felt so hard and sore and fuck, knees jerking, pearls onto her carpet, the hish stopped, he dressed, hurry, rubbed it in with his foot, hurry, took a deep breath, hurry, hurry, hurry.

Gasping, empty, sated.

A couple of weeks afterwards, and not being able to stop thinking about it, he went to House of Fraser to buy some underwear. It's my girlfriend's birthday. I thought I'd buy her something, well, you know. Yes, black. Her size? Oh, 38B.

He saw tights stuffed with rice. Saw balloons filled with water.

And when she said she couldn't bear to look at him any more, he realized how much she resembled Cynthia Chester.

Same tobacco-blonde hair and Malteser eyes.

Same ultimate unavailability.

When he was a teenager, he used to climb the tree at the bottom of Cynthia's garden, down by the beck, and watch her windows through the halo of his parka hood. He'd go over the times she'd cut his hair in the salon, her hands on his shoulders, nails long and painted a deep scarlet red. How he'd close his eyes and inhale the scent from her wrist as her fingers touched the skin of his neck.

And how it *thrilled*.

ANTONY PHONED THE PSYCH and left a message saying they were massively understaffed at the Day Centre and he couldn't make the session that Friday. Besides, Antony told himself, it was the manageress' last day and he wouldn't have missed her farewell bash for the whole world.

Some of the clients, those who were high on medication, blubbed a little, and when they gave her the leaving card and presents she went,

— Thank thank thank you so so much ev-everyone.

Antony whispered,

— Fare-fare-fucking well.

At least Spooner made an effort with the clients – he'd even helped clean Lerch that morning. Mother of Dog! He seemed full of new ideas and energy and commitment.

The staff had given him three months until he cracked.

WHEN HE GOT HOME that evening he found Jade on his doorstep, eyes tear-pink.

He stood before her, arms folded.

— How'd you find out where I lived?

She told him she'd dumped The Guy From The Village.

Antony felt a twinge of triumph, and a little explosion of guilt.

She wiped her face.

— He was a wanker anyway. Only interested in one thing.
Which meant, of course, that he'd got it.

She laughed, rubbing her nose on her sleeve.

— The back of your Valentine's card, idiot.

— Eh?

— You'd put SENDER. Fucks the whole Anonymous Admirer thing.

— I didn't.

He knew he had, he just hadn't expected her to turn up uninvited like this.

Or maybe he had.

It started to spit. They stared at each other.

— What's wrong?

— I can't, he said.

— You don't have any bodies in there, do you?

His larynx was a fat cauliflower, but a voice in his head said: Fuck it.

HE SAW THE INTERIOR through Jade's eyes, remembering Rebecca finding the dresses and his make-up box. Her reaction. The whole Kiss-Goodbye-To-Everything moment. He felt as if his life would be forever divided. And here he was, opening himself to rejection again. But Jade didn't seem to notice. She was nattering on about applying for university, and it surprised him – this sudden need to be exposed.

Then she pulled something from the chair and held it in front of her face.

A synthetic, jet-black wig hair.

Her eyes darted around the room.

The montage of women's faces;

The huge stack of women's magazines;

His charcoal drawings of Rebecca;

The open closet door;

The dresser full of make-up.

She chewed her cheeks quickly. Antony experienced mild emotional shock.

— You didn't tell me you had a flatmate, she said.

He stood in his room and looked at her and shrugged.

She put her hand to her mouth.

— I'm sorry. You're seeing someone else? I didn't think to ask. Sorry.

History repeating: his mess spilling into her life.

He shook his head and watched her confusion turn to anger.

— Well fucking *what* then?

He'd been telling a stranger his innermost secrets for months now, and yet he couldn't tell the person he felt closest to in life. It was pathetic. But what was he to say? That there's a woman that slides in and out of his life and she's always close by, if not entirely there. Trying to work out all of Jade's possible, probable responses.

— Sometimes, he said. Sometimes I like dressing up in women's clothes.

He said it so quietly, hesitantly, because he never thought he'd utter those words again. He never thought they'd spill from his head into another's and create a reaction that had no U-turn, no reversal.

Jade's eyes turned inward.

— But that's all, Jade. That's all.

She stood up quickly and he closed his eyes, flinched, steeling himself for a slap.

Heard the front door slam shut.

HE LIT A J and sat at his desk. The laptop hummed beneath his fingers and the modem flickered. The pixellated women were pink and ever-ready moist. Analysing the pictures, he found that some images always got him off, but mostly they just looked gorgeous for twenty seconds of intense pleasure and then looked really stupid. Trying to rationalize his physical and emotional needs – he'd spent so long trying to separate the two of them out that he didn't know whether he'd be able to piece them back together again. The vodka burned his heart and he ached with regret as he saw himself: a leering, stoned freak hunched over his laptop, trousers around his ankles, pretending everything in the world was hunky-fucking-dory and that he hadn't just lost the woman he loved.

SOME GENUS OF APPREHENSION crackled in Jack's voice.

— It's your mum, son.

— What about her?

— I'm sorry.

— . . .

— I don't think she's got long left.

He heard Jack swallow hard and so he said,

— Oh.

— She said she wants to see you.

Antony hung up and examined his hands; they were Jack's hands. He walked over to the window and looked at the city outside; so alien. He opened the closet door and looked at the clothes pole inside and saw his limp, ashen body hanging from it – his flayed skin hanging in sleavings, like a Bacon painting.

HE OPENED HIS WINDOW and listened to Manchester's consumptive wheeze: tyres hishing along Cheetham Hill, a tram shunting softly towards Victoria, the tuneless carol of a karaoke singer belting out of a pub, builders on a floodlit scaffold raising the city skyward. A siren, a child crying, children screaming in the park, the muffled applause of birds scattering. He could tell they were pigeons by the taut creak of their wings.

There was once a time he was interested in such things.

He remembered the rollers a-rolling and tumblers a-tumbling, how the birds would fall and shoot across the sky, somersaulting as if in celebration of his arrival. When he closed his eyes, he could still see the dark hexagonal shape of Eddie's dovecote, the weathervane on top rusted into SW. Eddie would be sat in his wicker chair inside, Sonny wagging his tail on the floor beside him.

He tried to remember the various types of dove and their differing calls. His favourites were the three-syllable *kwoo-hoo-cuc* of the collared, and the cadging whoop of the mourning dove: *Noah! Pay me! Pay me!*

Ada couldn't cope with Eddie in those last few months; he kept falling out of bed in the middle of the night and couldn't get up again. Talking to folk not there. Pointing. Cooing like one of his doves.

— Come help, lad. He's on the floor again.

Hands flapping. Blithering.

— Help. Please.

Eddie's face became so blade-thin, his hands shafts of bone, the paper-rustle of him on his deathbed, but his eyes remained bird-bright.

Antony wanted to unwind time, wanted to touch him again, to hear the music of Eddie's joyous bassoon laugh.

Val's face at Eddie's funeral, like she had nothing left.

ANTONY REMEMBERED Val's kids being taken away, one after the other.

Mikey, Barry, Lily.

Lily was the last to go. She was only a few years older than Antony, but when he screwed his eyes up tight and tried to remember her face, he couldn't. He remembered the nickname she'd given him though: Spug. Because he loved birds so much.

Her scratchy voice, full of wires and string. Her screams

before she started to fit, that cacophony of vowels and white noise. Little Spuggy. Sparrow boy. Lily. Feral fitting girl. The pissy smell of her. He remembered how terrifying it was seeing her hurly-burly. That unmistakable sound, a liquid hollow sound, of a human skull hitting the concrete. Her body churning, shambling, gyrating – how life would take a sudden detour. Like there was some enormous struggle going on inside her body and she always lost the fight.

She didn't have epilepsy; it had her.

— Little Spug.

The day she was taken away. The jealousy he felt.

Lily had escaped.

HE DIALLED THE NUMBER. He wasn't expecting anyone to answer. Truth was, he wanted to listen to his mother's voice on the answer machine, but a woman went,

— Hello?

— It's Antony.

Her voice fell, shifted. She told him his mother was in hospital.

— Who are you? Antony asked.

— Your mum's partner. My name's Hat.

— Hat?

— Hattie.

— Well, Hattie, as I'm sure you're aware, we haven't spoken for years. Are you sure she wants to see me?

— She's very ill, son.

— Don't call me son. How ill is ill?

— She's in theatre this afternoon.

Hattie struggled for breath.

— She really . . .

Antony got the name of the hospital and hung up.

HE LOOKED at the photograph of the young woman who was his mother. He opened drawers and moved things around inside as he left a message at the Day Centre, and then he phoned Jade, fingering a dress on his bed.

Hi, this is Jade. Don't be a stranger, leave a message . . .

He told her voicemail about his mother, about Cornwall.

He told her voicemail how he really, really needed her right now.

— I don't think I can handle this alone, he said. I need you, Jade.

He walked back over to his mother's photograph and placed a finger against her face, thinking *please*.

VI

BESIDE THE ROAD the theatre of spring had emerged, flora and fauna warming to life. He knew that the winter sky would start moving away now, stop being so close and heavy in the city. He loved the first days of spring and he could see them clearly in his mind: the springtime hailers, swifts and swallows darting around the gable ends, dive-bombing insects, skirling over the canals: *Apus apus* and *Hirundo rustica*, black specks in the blue. And the pinky froth-candles on the horse chestnuts, and how shadows would grow longer.

He closed his eyes and saw his home town, the valleys breathing with life, the pastured hills dotted with black doughnuts of wrapped silage bags, Swarth Coum's slopes smocked with wildflowers and sprouting sedge and fluffy bog cotton. He missed the intensity of the changing of the seasons in the country, how it made you feel meek, inconsequential. How shattering it could be.

HE LOOKED AT THE birthday card from his mother and Hattie on the mantelpiece. Inside, Hattie had written how wonderful it was for his mother to have him back in her life.

Hattie kept calling him son; it made him scream inside his skull.

The first weekend he went down to Cornwall, when he visited his mother in the liver unit and saw her wired up, slipping in and out of consciousness, he felt the coldness of his blood. The light dimmed, his ears whistled, and yet he was completely clear-headed.

He sat beside her those first two days, seething.

Hattie kept inviting him to stay at their cottage in Mevagissey, but he didn't want to see the place where his mother had been happy.

Spooner said he could take some compassionate leave; that was the week she died. She juddered like an epileptic and the doctors bustled him from the room. Antony watched through the window, how her body arched and heaved under the paddles. He saw sparks; but they brought her back.

The third time he went down she was conscious. Nothing could have prepared him for it: her cirrhosis-yellow eyes and tallow skin; the scattered Kleenexes full of bloodied oysters. But the worst thing was her distended stomach – she looked pregnant.

They stared at each other for a long time.

— What do you think to Hattie?

He tutted and she coughed wetly. He passed her some tissues.

— Lou, he said quietly. She made my life hell.

His mother spat; Antony inhaled the stench of organ failure. Her eyes looked spaced as she went,

— I know.

HATTIE FILLED him in: after Lou had left – she'd had an affair and moved to Newcastle to be with her new girlfriend – his mother had decided to go to Cornwall to try and dry herself out. She tried some aversion therapy, some drug that caused her to puke whenever she drank, but it didn't work. Then she joined the local AA and that's where they met. His mother was already suffering from toxaemia and chronic pancreatitis and there was some nerve damage to her legs and signs of heart damage. Cardiomyopathy. But it was the internal bleeding that got her in the end. And the irony of it was, she'd been dry for six months. On the wagon.

Antony knew all about her wagon.

The chief physician told him,

— There'll be no recovery.

Meaning she was drowning in her own blood.

So they were releasing her to be with Hattie, to die in familiar surroundings. They were loading her up with a morphine drip, unspoken but implicit: a final dose. Hattie was going to give him *the call*, but he'd already said his goodbyes six years ago.

HE PLACED THE DICTAPHONE on his dressing table and pressed play.

He'd been to see the psych a few times after his confession, but the more they deliberated Antony's secret life, the stronger his emotional responses of fear and self-loathing. He hadn't been for the past two weeks, and he knew he'd never return. But he kept listening to the recordings, searching for something.

He could hear his footsteps as he walked along the corridor, the muffle of fabric as he sat down. The nasal tone of his voice, how his accent had changed: vowels flatter, elongated. He was picking up a Mancunian accent.

After a minute of usual pleasantries, the psych launched in,
— Your efforts with Kenneth might be making your depression worse because the goal is blocked. Perhaps it's unachievable, and your depression means you might find it hard to give up on this goal. Maybe you need to stop distracting yourself?

Antony had told him in the previous session about finding out where Kenneth's old parish was in Chester, and that he'd made contact with one of his old flock, some cranky old bird that cleaned the church. She'd told Antony about how wonderful Kenneth was as a priest. There was a 'but' though: he had his affair.

The psych failed to stifle a yawn.

— We need to start talking about your cross-dressing.

The scratchy sound of Antony shrugging.

— It's persistent, recurrent. It's habitual. You told me you've done it a few times without the breath play. Have you ever thought that these may be very separate issues?

— No. I haven't.

— And there's an issue of hostility here.

— Towards whom?

— You tell me?

A pause.

— We need to look at what motivates you. Perhaps you could tell me about what you think about while you're doing this. Your fantasies.

— Why?

— Because what you're doing is potentially lethal.

— And?

— And we need to find out what's hidden in your actions.

The sound of their voices filled Antony's flat. He closed his eyes and saw himself in the mirror, strapping his cock into the gluteal folds.

— I'm a pervert?

— That's not helpful.

— Does this mean I'm a psycho?

— Your depression is non-psychotic.

— Is the depression causing it?

— What exactly do you think about when you're doing this?

Another crackled, muffled section. Then the psych's voice,

— So it's a confrontation?

— I guess.

— Between you and your mother?

— No. Jesus.

— So the woman in the mirror, does she have a name?

— No.

— Why not?

The hiss of silence.

— How do you feel about the woman in the mirror?

Flexing its muscles.

— What does she represent to you?

— I think she's beautiful.

— OK.

— Stunning.

— Anything else?

— She's my, I don't know.

Like she was listening.

— You idealize her?

— Suppose.

— What do skirts and heels represent to you, Antony?

Without hesitation,

— Invincibility.

■ Stop « Rewind

He listened again, the voice no longer sounding like his.

HE FOUND KENNETH crouched on his bedroom floor, moving pieces of paper around.

— Where's Lizzie?

— She's just left, mate.

— Course course.

Kenneth had started to group the words and images together.

Antony asked,

— What do they mean?

Kenneth pointed at the largest collection.

— These here are my ma and pa and my childhood in Stoke. These here are me and Lizzie. These are you, cunt-features. And these? He clicked his fingers. These are what I can make of this fucking dump.

He pointed to the centre of the carpet: a large space with the single word BABY inside it. He looked at Antony.

— I want you to help me fill this in.

Antony sat beside him on the bed.

— Do you remember anything about being a priest, Kenneth?

Kenneth snorted.

— You're joking?

— I'm not.

— Jesus. I must've been out of my fucking mind.

187

Antony pointed to the sign above the headboard.

— What's 'DREAM OF MAKING' mean?

Kenneth stood up and pulled it off the wall, placing it in the centre of the carpet, next to the word BABY.

He began to stammer.

— You tell me, f-f-fucking Mastermind.

THAT NIGHT was Antony's birthday bash at Gino's in the Northern Quarter. Jade and John and Moon were coming, but Nurse Bog Breath wouldn't release Kenneth for the evening.

Antony and Jade, on the scant occasions they'd spoken to each other, hadn't discussed The Day At The Flat. He was surprised she was still talking to him, but something had definitely changed. Her tone when she spoke to him: woebegone, full of burden. He resented her pity, but without her in his life, felt he'd have nothing to cling to. She sounded upbeat when she called. Said she had some good news.

— I don't want to steal your thunder, she said, but you'll have to wait till tonight.

HATTIE TOLD HIM how his mother kept making trivial recoveries.

— She's heavily medicated. She sleeps most of the time. You could still come, though. She'll know that you're here. She'll sense it.

Six and a half hours on the train to St Austell to watch her drown in blood?

— I'll come when it's time, he said.

STANDING NAKED in front of the mirror when 'Vicious' started trilling away on his mobile. There was no hello how are you?

— Mum still has friends in Chester, you know.

Sarah. He cuffed a hand over his balls.

188

— Right.

— She knows you've been doing some snooping around.

— Hmm.

— You're an interfering bastard.

— . . .

— Mum wanted to ring you herself, but she's too upset.

— Listen, I never meant . . .

— In fact, we both think you should stop seeing Dad altogether.

He knew it was a risk,

— You know you have a half-sister?

— . . .

— Sorry.

— I want *nothing* to do with her. Nor does Mum. Get it?

And as he listened to the dead tone, Antony thought about his own half-brother in Spain. He wished he'd told Sarah he knew how she felt.

He dressed and sat in his chair, smoking, wondering about his antidepressants.

Thinking what a waste of fucking time.

JADE'S GOOD NEWS? She'd secured a place at Durham University that October, studying history and politics. As she told Antony, he saw that she wasn't wearing the jade bracelet he'd bought her for Christmas and he hated himself. Then she gave him his birthday present: a framed photograph of them both, taken at the party at her house, their sweaty faces pressed together, eyes deep with chemical love. He remembered holding her till she fell asleep that morning, and then curling up on the floor beside her.

It was a sign, he told himself. I'm winning her back.

He kept the photograph next to his bed.

He kissed her face before he went to sleep at night.

ANTONY LOOKED OUT at the city and realized he'd absent-mindedly smoked half a J when his mobile buzzed across the top of the TV.

Jade.

The text said simply: I miss you.

It put him in such a black mood. It was a mystery to him. It was a gift he didn't ask for. She was under his skin. Did *I miss you* = I love you, or did *I miss you* = I pity you? Love, making him feel only half-human. Sex and emotion, the messy glue of wholeness. Love, as far as he was concerned, just went and fucked everything. Soon as he had Rebecca, he lost himself, lost her friendship, lost his joy in her. And it was happening all over again with Jade. But who did she miss anyway? Who she thought he was? The person she met last year? The person she liked before she saw his room and the things he did in there? That night on Swarth Coum – he felt like he'd been cursed ever since.

The weed took him even closer to the darkside.

He put the photograph of them both in a drawer and then went into the bathroom and popped the little orange Mirtaza-pine pills out of their foil, watching them spin in the flush of the toilet bowl. Goodbye, antidepressants.

He was afraid his life was becoming synthetic.

He wanted to feel alive.

HATTIE HUGGED HIM ON the doorstep and thanked him for coming.

— Rita's loaded. Don't be surprised by her perkiness.

He opened the bedroom door to that sickening uric stench. His mother frowned. She'd aged twenty years in the past two weeks. Grown smaller. Her grey hair had been cut short and her face and hand muscles juddered; the life in her, flickering. It was as if he was seeing her for the first time and her illness had put them on an equal footing, because there was a look of collusion in her eyes. OK. You win.

He sat down.

The terrifying IV bag hung between them, feeding her morphine with its eerie drip.

Click-click. The button in her hand — how she kept squeezing it.

He was surprised to see a photograph of himself on the wall, taken during his first year at high school. The maroon V-neck. The gold and black stripy tie. The basin-cut.

— You never kept any photos of me at home when I was little.

She laughed sleepily,

— You kept taking them down.

Her voice frayed, tattered, torn.

Hattie popped her head around the door.

— Can I get you anything?

His mother shook her head slowly.

— OK. Just give me a shout.

After a moment his mother inflected croakily,

— You like her, don't you?

Antony nodded.

— Better than Lou, eh?

— Anyone's fucking better than Lou.

The rotten stumps of her teeth as she laughed.

— How come you hated Jack so much?

He hadn't planned to say anything; if he could, he'd take it back.

— Fuck sake, lad.

She rummaged under her covers and handed him a pouch of DRUM tobacco.

— I'm gasping. Do us a rollie, quick-sharp. Hattie comes in, tek it.

He looked at the IV bag.

— Meks no difference now, she wheezed.

He rolled the rollie. His hands were shaking. Lit it. Passed it across.

— So how come, he said, you're still in touch with him?

She exhaled, releasing a smile.

— He rings once or twice a year. Guilt. Hattie talks to him, not me.

— Why's that?

Click-click. Her eyes widened and back straightened. She had a smidgen of a smirk on her face, like she was nourishing some secret joke.

— It were you that wanted to meet him, laddo. I told you what a waste of space he is. But oh no, little clever sod that you are. So honestly then, is your life better or worse for knowing him? Come on, tell me.

He heard what she was saying, but not what she was telling him.

— Not all men are bastards, Mam.

She smiled.

— It's lucky I had Eddie in my life, he said. It's lucky I had some normality.

She seemed to disappear into the cushions.

— Val's little drinking buddy, eh?

— What?

— You *know* what.

He stared at the wall, shrugged. She went,

— Oh, there's *lots* of stuff I know about. Like you being a knicker-thief. Like you sniffing glue at school. Like you burning the church to the ground. Like you being a selfish little bastard all your life.

He stood up and went to the window.

He hadn't thought about the church in years. He remembered the high pulpit where the red-faced priest had stood, mouth spittle-wet, neck tendons protruding. The church a-murmur with it. Whores of the daughters of Israel. His mother dragging him down the aisle out of the church, the hard pull of her, and how he'd looked back and seen the piercing blue iris of the church clock. And he remembered walking the streets of the town afterwards, wondering whose eyes had been watching that night. The whispering town. Like they suddenly had permission from God.

Outside, the garden led to a field of wind-bent tress, and beyond the field was the choppy grey sea.

He pictured them walking along the beach together.

He pictured them in a small boat, sailing away.

— Here, she said.

He took the rollie off her. She went,

— I heard you the other day.

She held his gaze.

— I heard what you said to me.

Click-click.

— So why'd you let Lou beat me?

194

— Because you deserved it.

— You should've protected me.

— You should've behaved yourself.

— And why'd I always have to lie for you?

— About what?

— Being a dyke.

He remembered Locky then, the school bully pinning him to the wall outside of school, his hands around Antony's neck and how Antony had willed his eyes to betray the pain inside, smiling into Locky's face. It was the same look his mother had now.

We're so alike, he thought.

— The whole town knew, but you *always* denied it.

— That was *my* business, she said.

— The people in that town made my life hell.

— Don't exaggerate.

— I had the shit kicked out of me for years, he said. I was ostracized because of *your* sexuality, and you didn't have the decency to come out to me. But I knew everything.

— You ashamed of me?

— You were ashamed of yourself, that's the whole fucking problem.

She wiped her slack face, click-clicking rapidly.

— Lad, you were nowt but trouble from the day you were born. Now if you've nothing better to say, then why don't you give me some bastard peace. For once.

He saw a calmness in her eyes that he'd never seen before.

He leaned down and kissed her cheek quickly.

She opened her arms a little, but turned into her pillows.

Made a noise.

THAT NIGHT AT THE Bay View B&B, he sat in his room thinking: Nothing better to say?

What he wanted to say was,

— Please don't die.

What he wanted to say was,

— Let's make a fresh start.

But he was scared she'd laugh in his face.

HE WAS ON THE platform at St Austell when Hattie phoned. She said they'd administered the final dose together early that morning and that his mother went peacefully.

— Would you like to come and see her?

He really wanted to feel something.

— No.

— She wants you to scatter her ashes.

— Oh?

— Up on Swarth Coum.

It shocked him.

The train pulled into the station.

— I need to go, Hattie. I'll phone later.

He took a deep breath and said,

— Thank you.

VII

VII

VI.

It was 8:21 a.m. and he'd failed to engage with the photonic mong-inducing flux of the TV. Sleep was in another hemisphere, another time zone, another season, another bed – it was another body sweating in a hot room as a soft breeze gently stirred the curtains and cicadas strummed a soft vibrato outside.

He wondered what was behind this need of Jade's to know everything, to delve, to share, to make connections that weren't really there. He found himself wanting to lie, to create a new biography. He felt explosive and hated what was inside his head. He'd had the past two days off work, building up his sleep-debt, but thoughts and images tumbled through his mind and he couldn't make them stop. That dead hour between three and four a.m. was the worst – the weird, ghostly silence of the city – it made him feel like the last man on Earth, that he was lost in time, experiencing suspended animation. He made a note to himself: go to the clinic today and fill in a repeat prescription form. He needed the Mirtazapine, the sweet narcosis of M. The comfort of sleep.

For some reason he lied to her,
— Mother's OK, thanks.

He could tell Jade was in a bar somewhere, and maybe it was alcohol but something in her voice had changed. A remoteness.

But then she invited him – under duress, he felt – to Pete and Eileen's for tea the following week. He gathered she hadn't blabbed to them: by the way, Antony's not the man you think he is. He likes wearing dresses and hanging himself for kicks; but it's not *a problem*, it's not *an issue*.

— Eileen said you're more than welcome to bring Kenneth along.

— Really?

— Really.

— Thank you, Jade.

— For what?

He whispered a demonstrative,

— Everything.

She cleared her throat and hung up.

HE DISCOVERED he hardly knew his mother at all. She'd changed a lot over the past few years; mellowed, become interested in life. Hattie told him they'd even been planning to get married when they changed the laws.

— Great, he said. My two step-mums.

Hattie was upset he didn't want to be at the crematorium.

— Mother was an atheist, he said. What would she care?

— Well, I'm coming up to Manchester in a couple of weeks, whether you like it or not. To give you the urn in person. It's only right.

— You can send it by Parcel Force.

— Will it ever end?

Her anger shocked him.

— What?

— Your hostility towards Rita.

He swallowed audibly.

— I hope so.

MOTHER KNEW so much. The church. His glue-sniffing.

A name shot into his brain like adrenalin.

Cynthia.

His patience had paid off. One night, her bedroom light came on and he spotted her long yellow hair. He puckered his mouth, kissed the back of his hand. She walked over to her bed; she wasn't wearing any knickers. He pressed himself into the tree. *Oh Cynthia.* The image of her nakedness was so unMotherlike – belly flat, hips narrow. He pulled his cock out into the cool night air, unfurling into hardness as her arms rose into a pink dressing gown and she turned, moving towards the window. But she drew the curtains and faded to a silhouette.

The dark circle of nipple, the fuzz of pubic – that's all he wanted.

Or better still, to see her unbuttoning slowly.

Then he saw the billow of clothes on her washing line. Brightly coloured, near-human shapes. Bras. Knickers. Limbless tights. Waiting for her body.

He sneaked across her lawn and then away into the night.

And so it began: the consummation of his fantasy; the rough feminization of the boy in the mirror; impersonating the girl that slipped in and out of his life.

Observing, mimicking, invoking, denying.

The confusion of it all had only just begun.

KENNETH HAD LOCKED himself in his room and then forgotten why.

Nurse Bog Breath showed Antony the letter.

Lizzie was filing for divorce.

Nurse Bog Breath placed a hand on Antony's shoulder.

— Fuck them, he said.

HE PRESSED PLAY on his Dictaphone, picked up his glass and stood before the mirror.

— Perhaps your fantasies are a way of preserving your masculinity?

— I'm not sure.

— Over and over again, you succeed. Survive the trauma they put you through.

He sipped the vodka, turned his head slowly, pouting.

— I'm talking about being made to feel bad for being a boy, a young male.

— I guess.

Lit from above, his cheekbones looked so prominent. He licked his lips and tried to smile; he had the same crow's-feet laughter-lines as his mother.

— What's the one thing your mother and Lou lacked?

There was a long pause. Antony stepped back from the mirror and twisted his body, throwing his hair over a shoulder.

— Femininity?

— And?

— Affection. Warmth. Love.

— And?

He ran a hand up his leg and over his arse.

— Cocks.

— But *you* have a cock.

— Are we still talking about this?

Another drawn-out silence during which a child can be heard crying in the corridor outside the therapy room. Bad timing.

Antony put his drink on the mantelpiece and sat in his chair, listening.

— You dress to disguise your masculinity. And then you imagine they try to overpower you, they try to kill you. But ultimately you win because you survive, and you are potent because you have a penis and you can masturbate and ejaculate.

Thinking he wouldn't have had such a conversation with a woman.

— Yes, Antony's voice said. But I have to.

Antony turned the laptop off, lay down, and closed his eyes.

With the strenuous shunt of his heart in his ears, he remembered the train journey back from Cornwall, watching the tracks as they extended into the distance where everything appeared to meet, and it felt like his life was going in reverse, that he was always travelling in the wrong direction. Train stations, waiting for it all to begin, to end.

They were all dead. Eddie. Val. Mother.

No one left.

He wondered if this might tell him something.

HE FOUND the old woman in the church again. That woody, churchy smell – he could feel the tug of his mother's hand. Could almost see the glowering eyes above the pews.

He walked through fractals of coloured light. Jesus, Mary, Joseph. Saints in dark niches, banks of semi-melted candles, effigies rigid with godliness. Flowers in the font and carvings of ancient knights. The large stone columns twisting upwards, the ceiling vaulted like the tail of a fantail dove.

He stood in the church, his eyes adjusting to bars of coloured light, and let the childhood memories wash over him.

The old woman seemed pleased to see him. She asked after Kenneth; Antony told her he'd been ill, about the amnesia.

— So I'm trying to find the woman, Antony said. The one he had the affair with.

The old woman sat on a pew and drummed her fingers on her knees.

— Isn't forgiveness a Christian tenet?

She looked vexed.

— My husband died of Alzheimer's last year. It pains me to admit it, but it was like a relief when he passed.

— I'm really sorry to hear that.

She looked up at him with milky, glistening eyes.

— Why do you want to find her?

— Because other than me he has no one left.
— What about Elizabeth?
— She's filing for divorce.
— Oh no. No-o. That's terrible.
— Yes. It is.
— That's the trouble nowadays.
— What is?
— No values.
— I'm not here to judge. I just want this woman's name.

She shrugged, tutted, sighed. Shook her old grey head.

WHEN HE GOT home he booted up and went to the BT.com website. He typed in the woman's surname and initial, and then the name of the village.

SEARCHED FOR CAPE, J, IN AND AROUND CHRISTLETON.

Jackpot: an address and telephone number.

All day he'd been wondering what to say, how to open the conversation without totally freaking her out. What if her daughter answered? What if she was married and her husband was a jealous psycho? What if, what if?

He pressed the number.
— You'll have to speak up.
— Kenneth, he shouted. I'm a friend of Kenneth's.
— Yes?
— My name's Antony.
— What's happened?
— He's in a care unit. Lizzie's filing for divorce.

He listened to her breathe for a long five seconds.
— Give me the address.
— Be prepared, he said. He won't remember you.

DEAR ANTONY,

    I am sorry not to have seen you for your last few appoint-
ments with me. I hope that things are OK with you? If you
wish to arrange another appointment with me, please contact
me at the above address. You may have decided that you no
longer wish to attend sessions with me, but should you change
your mind in the future, please do not hesitate to contact me
and we can arrange a time to meet.

    With best wishes . . .

He ripped the letter in half and dropped it in the bin.

THE CHILL BATHROOM, knickers around her ankles, his mother looked at him, groaned, and then lowered her head.

— Need to pee, he said.

He walked around the side of her as she shuffled forward.

The shutters of her eyes were down. They were silent together. The lino was chilly beneath his bare feet and the stench of her booze-breath was sickly sweet as he trickled and splashed behind her.

Later, the wind began blowing as if the planet had become unhinged. Wind whistling along the window ledge, howling across the gables, coughing through the trees. He climbed out of his bed and whispered into her room.

Lou had gone again. Blood on the walls.

But he knew she'd be back.

Broad-backed Mam.

He moved alongside her, trying not to look at the large, flat breasts hanging down her sides. Trying not to look at the dark uneven oval around the blunt nub of each nipple, blue veins running away from them in broken streams. And the thought: I fed from those once. He found it hard to imagine.

He wanted to climb in beside her, to snuggle into warm, heavy flesh. To feel the consoling weight of her. To know that she loved him and he loved her. That immutable touch that says simply: I love you. I will let nothing happen to you.

But she recoiled whenever he touched her.

The silvery hue coming though the window made her look younger, like the girl he kept in his back pocket.

He looked at her for a long time before pulling the bed-sheet up a little.

And then a little more.

WHEN HE WOKE, he could still see her mean lips.

Her eyes like hot coals.

KENNETH'S LANGUAGE was as flowery as ever, but he remained relatively sober and Antony realized what an expert he was at improvising in new situations with complete strangers. Antony asked Pete to put The Who on the stereo and Kenneth repeated the same lewd jokes Antony had heard a thousand times before. They had the courtesy to humour him and laugh at the right points, though there were a few times they slipped up and started quizzing him about The Past. Antony thought Kenneth would get upset. Where is she? Where's my Lizzie? But he just chain-smoked his way through the meal and looked around the room every two minutes to remind himself where he was.

Then he saw a piece of paper sticking out of Kenneth's jacket pocket.

The word: FORGET.

Pete and Kenneth headed into the lounge to admire his vinyl collection.

Eileen approached Antony in the kitchen.

— I have a lot of respect for what you do. You really care for him, don't you?

Antony started welling up. He wanted to tell her everything.

— I do.

— You're so patient.

And behind him Jade said,

— Yes, he is.

Antony excused himself and nipped upstairs to the loo. He took a quick peek in Jade's old bedroom. Suitcases. Poster tubes. CDs in boxes.

She was packing for university.

— ANT, you OK?

He blew his nose and opened the bathroom door.

— What is it?

She pulled him into her bedroom.

— My mother's dead.

— Oh, Ant.

He felt so ugly inside.

— She's gone and drunk herself to death and I . . .

Her eyes softened into his. Tenderly she touched his cheek. He flinched.

A car blasted its horn outside. He looked at his watch: the cab driver.

— I'm so sorry, Ant.

— How's my face?

— When did you find out?

— You can't tell I've been beefing?

— Come here.

Ignoring her open arms, he glanced around for a mirror, but then couldn't bring himself to look at his reflection, scared of what he'd see. He straightened his hair with her brush, tied it back, and headed back down the stairs. She repeated his name behind him.

Downstairs, they were engaged in a raucous round of *Shit Scrabble Fuck*.

Kenneth didn't want to leave. Pete and Eileen said they'd had such a good time and that he was to bring Kenneth around again whenever he wanted. Eileen asked him if he was OK.

He had to get out of there.

He took Kenneth's arm down the garden path and helped him into the cab.

Jade followed them out.

— Ant, do you want me to come with you? Do you want to stay? Ant?

He tried, but failed, to smile at her through the windscreen.

KENNETH STARED at him from the doorway and Antony wondered if contacting Julia was the wrong thing to do, if perhaps she would only make the situation worse. He wanted to save Kenneth, to make his life better, to change the way Kenneth saw the world, to create new memories, better memories for him to live by. But he knew it was hopeless.

Antony and Kenneth moved into each other, embracing tightly. It was just like the first time Eddie held him. The first time he'd ever been held by a man.

They broke away awkwardly, their eyes carrying the same implicit message.

HE WATCHED HATTIE WALK towards him along the platform. She kissed his cheek and put her arm through his.

— I need a drink.

They went to the Station Inn and when Antony was at the bar he saw her fiddling with her bag and he thought: not here. He took the drinks over and there she was: his mother in a rectangular, white plastic box, sitting on the table.

Hattie raised her glass into the air.

— To Rita.

They chinged glasses and he took a heavy mouthful and saw the image of a cardboard coffin with the word HEAD printed at one end. He saw the cremator flicking the temperature gauge before sliding his mother into the retort.

He downed his vodka in one.

— Want another?

He didn't wait for a reply. He went to the bar and bought two more drinks.

He felt giddy. Wanted to laugh out loud.

Hattie touched his hand as he sat back down.

— Why didn't you come?

— She was an atheist.

— So you keep saying.

— She wouldn't have cared. Trust me.

— She wanted to contact you, six months ago. There was talk of her having a split liver transplant.

— I don't think anyone would want my liver.

The fade of Hattie's ebullient beam – it made something dim inside of him.

— Really? You wouldn't give your own mother? To save her life?

He tried not to raise his voice,

— No.

Hattie rummaged in her bag and pulled something out.

— Rita wanted you to have this.

She slapped a black book down. A D D R E S S E S.

He opened it and the school photo of him dropped out.

— Why'd she leave me this?

Hattie necked her drink, shrugged.

— Haven't the foggiest. It was all she seemed to have.

He flicked through the names and addresses and phone numbers.

Each of them had lines through.

— Thanks.

She nodded at the drinks.

— I shouldn't be doing this. I'm on a new program: Moderation Management. But I can't . . .

Antony put a hand on her shoulder and watched her heave.

— Let's make this the last one, eh?

She pulled a hanky from her sleeve and blew her nose loudly. He went,

— How long are you here for?

— I'm heading to Scotland first thing, to see my brother and his family. I can't be on my own right now.

He wanted to tell her that he'd stay with her in Cornwall. He'd be company.

— Thank you, he said.

She rubbed her eyes.

— For what?

— For giving Mother something she never had before.

Hattie put her hand on his.

— She never stopped loving you. Despite everything.

— Why Swarth Coum?

Hattie stared into the bottom of her empty glass.

— Hattie?

— I don't know. Here.

She handed him a piece of paper.

— The certificate from the crematorium, thought you might like it.

Then she pulled a goldy heart-shaped locket from inside her blouse.

— It's a keepsake, she said. I was wondering if you'd mind.

She eyed the plastic box.

— Help yourself, he said.

She dabbed her eyes and took the box into the Ladies.

He pictured her taking a pinch of his mother's cremains.

Pictured her snorting Mother like cocaine.

HE WALKED HER back to her hotel and then he milled absentmindedly around the Northern Quarter until a rat-faced junkie shoved a Styrofoam cup into his face.

— Any change, chief?

Antony saw tar-coated teeth. Saw pupils pinned.

— I need all my change, Antony said, for fags and booze.

— CUUUUUNNNNNT!

Antony suddenly felt very awake.

He wandered around a few of the charity shops and bought a dress, a pair of skanky heels, a slaggy skirt and a cheap brunette wig. He almost left his mother in M&S when he was looking for some sheer tights and then realized she was dead and that he was carrying her around the Arndale Shopping Centre in a Tesco's carrier bag.

On the way home, he received a call.

— Why was that *woman* at the unit yesterday?

— Hello, Lizzie.

— Who the hell do you think you are?

— Kenneth won't remember her visit. He doesn't know who she is.

— That woman . . .

— Yet.

— She ruined our lives, you little bastard.

— You inviting Kenneth, then?

— You're going to regret this.

— Inviting him to your wedding?

— I'm coming down on you like a ton of bricks, boy.

— Bite me.

THE WHISTLING IN HIS EARS. The world freezes and there's a screaming in his head and it's so loud and intense it becomes the sibilant sound he hates so much.

Only one way to stop the noise.

Only one way to stop the pain.

The loop rises up, just below his jaw. He places a towel between his neck and the ligature to protect vessels, to avoid that give-away the herringbone pattern, that V-shape at the point of apposition.

Paroxysm of asphyxiation. Paroxysm of orgasm.

From the age of twelve, he was a man trapped inside a child's body, and he needed a different kind of love. But when you can't fuck someone else, you fuck yourself.

Sitting behind his desk at school, staring into the blankness of his head hour upon hour, hot and sweaty thinking about sex, how to do it and what it would feel like. The dull ache in the abdomen, the hot dizziness of testosterone, the constant churn of spunk.

Watching girls bloom and blossom before his eyes, breasts bulging, hips pushing against the too-tight uniforms. And the jealousy he felt, watching the sensuous sway of oestrogen. He wanted their blood. He hated the masculinization of his body. He wanted to be a little girly-boy forever.

He didn't have a cool hairdo, didn't wear the latest fashions, wasn't into weight-lifting, didn't knot his tie thinly, didn't care how he looked, wasn't into football or rugby, didn't get the jokes, didn't finger girls behind the swimming pool on Youth Club night, didn't go on school holidays, didn't call girls *frigid* or *goers* or *fishy knickers*. But by the time kids started congregating up the park on a Friday night, he was already drinking cider and beer and wine and sniffing glue on a daily basis. Scab moustache.

And he wore women's knickers to school under his uniform.

Living in a constantly altered state of consciousness, getting high, getting by, by whatever means. Glue, wanking, hanging, adrenalin and neuropeptides, all the same buzz and blur and numb and calm. Fighting back in his own way. All of his milk-round money spent in the hardware store. Tripping, he'd often find Jack sitting next to him on a branch in a tree, studying him slowly and shaking his head.

When he was fourteen, he brought her down off the moors and into town, walking the streets of the sleepy estate, scraping his heels along the footpaths, chewing chuddy like a little scrubber, wishing someone would catch him, expose him.

When his mother and Lou were at their bars, he'd close his bedroom door and play heavy metal so loud the speakers would distort. Then he went through the whole routine of being beaten up and strangled, Val's nylon tights pulled as high as they could go, securing them with a belt.

He killed himself at night. It was, quite literally, *breathtaking*.

HE REMEMBERED SEARCHING the psych's face for a stain of revulsion.

— For you the inevitable and ultimate exposure equals pleasure, does it not?

Antony felt like a blank page. In a tiny voice he went,

— Yes.

SPOONER ASKED HIM if he could have a word in his office. He said he'd been pleased with what he'd seen of Antony's work recently and that he'd been reading his file and CV and thought Antony was capable of a lot more.

— I'd like to promote you to Assistant Manager.
— Jesus.
— Is that a yes?
— What about the other staff? Equal ops and all that?
— I'm offering you first refusal.
— But my life's very complicated.
— Really?
— I don't think I could handle the pressure right now.
— It'll mean less time-face with the clients.
— Time-face?
— Less hands-on.
— When could I start?
— There's just one thing.
— Oh?
— Your involvement with Kenneth.
— I see.
— Lizzie's been on to the Area Manager. We feel, well . . .

Antony stood up and showed his palms.
— Thanks. But no thanks.

SHE WAS IN her mid- to late-thirties and wasn't bad looking. Actually, she was quite fit. As Julia shook Antony's hand, Kenneth raised a lewd eyebrow behind her.

Nurse Bog Breath appeared in the doorway.

— Kenneth, if you insist on smoking, *please* do it in the garden.

She unhooked Kenneth's red anorak from the back of the door and took his arm.

— You must observe the House Rules. How many times?

— Mardy cow, Kenneth said, just loud enough for them all to hear.

Julia went to follow him but Antony stopped her.

— Can I have a word?

When Kenneth was out of earshot he went,

— He doesn't remember you?

She deflated.

— He keeps calling me 'nurse'. But I quite like the new Kenneth, despite the fact he's oblivious.

— Ah, oblivion.

She gave him a dirty look.

— Has your daughter been?

— Kerry? No.

— Does she know?

She sat on Kenneth's bed and ran a hand across his pillow. Antony tried to imagine the two of them together.

— It's terrible, she said. I'm such a bad, bad person.

Their clandestine electricity fizzing through the stuffy congregation.

— I considered telling her he died.

She looked at Antony with such sleepy eyes.

— I totally understand, he said.

— Lizzie told me I'd ruined her life. She called me an evil slut.

He took the picture frame apart and passed her the small Polaroid.

Her brow knotted. She turned it over and said,

— I gave it to him after Kerry was born.

She looked at him steadily.

— Is Kenneth playing games with us?

— Was Kerry a breech birth?

— Why?

— Was Kenneth there?

She nodded and went,

— That's when it all came out.

Antony thought he should have told her that Kenneth remembered.

A flashbulb.

She handed the Polaroid back.

— I'm sorry.

HE STARED OUT of his window at the city at night. He didn't know how to look at it, how to read such an enormous urban blur. He suddenly felt very lost.

He spoke to the window,

— What do I do?

All he got in response was TV laughter from the flat below. He made the mistake of listening to the recording again. The final meeting with the psych.

— In medical terms, the psych said, your breath play is known as asphyxiophilia, and I believe your cross-dressing may be mainly fetishistic.

Antony told himself his life would not be changed.

— Labels, at this stage, give us a framework to work within.

The psych then spoke about Antony's fantasies as a paraphilic script, and said his attraction to women's clothes was suggestive of transvestophilia. He told Antony how asphyxiation, how obstruction of the carotid artery, could potentially be lethal.

— It's OK, Antony heard himself saying. I'm always safe.

— Don't do what your mother did, Antony.

— What the fuck's that meant to mean?

— Don't deny yourself the right to be happy.

This was the point where Antony had stood up and shouted,

— It's my family that need therapy, not me. I'm the fucking

normal one because I came for help, but I get labelled fucking mental. Well, I don't *want* to be shrunk any more. I wanted to understand this twist in me, but you've made me feel even smaller. And I want to be A GIANT.

The psych had smiled compassionately and so Antony screamed,

— FUCK YOU!

Antony deleted all of the files on his Dictaphone, but as soon as he heard the chime sound-effect that indicated the files were well and truly gone, he regretted it.

HE TOOK a cab to his dealer's down by the canal, and when he got back he did a few lines and took his clothes off and stood in front of the mirror. He was naked but he could see her staring back, and his fear spelled one thing:

T-R-A-N-N-Y

So he smashed the four standing mirrors and ran at the walls, attacking the drawings of Rebecca, ripping them into shreds and jumping on them, screaming till the pain in his chest made tears roll. Then he put his fist through the door and kicked the television over and shattered the screen with his ashtray and smashed the video-recorder. Then he emptied his drawers and threw everything into the centre of the room: heels, skirts, CDs, books, duvet, pillows.

And then he tore the photographs of his mother and Jack to pieces.

He couldn't breathe. He didn't know what he was doing.

He went into the kitchen and pulled the bottles of vodka out of the freezer and listened to the dull *thwack* as they hit the concrete outside. Then he went into the bedroom and opened the window and lifted large armfuls of his stuff and threw it into the yard below. He emptied the suitcase out the window, his ligatures, his knots, and pushed his bed up against the wall and tried to pull the door off its hinges because he could feel it inside. Something.

He sat and heaved on the floor, looking into a broken shard of mirror, remembering the moment he felt her for the first time.

AFTER A WHILE none of the beatings came to matter. They happened to someone else. To the girl in the next room. The little girl his mother said she'd always wanted. But hers was the face he saw them beating. She took it for him. She took it all.

When he looked into the broken shard of mirror, he remembered that first time: pressing himself into the wall, listening to her sobbing in the next room. But then she stopped. He heard the pad of her footsteps. The door to his room opened and he closed his eyes and curled up with fear. But she climbed onto the bed and he felt her.

Felt her loving arms around him.

That's when she began interrupting his sleep; he'd wake and find her at the foot of his bed, her back to him. He'd beg her to turn around, fingers grasping at the bedroom air, but she'd always disappear. And so it spilled over into a desperate need.

Of wanting. Of not wanting.

HE WENT DOWN to his scattered world in the yard outside and set fire to it all. His earthly possessions went up in a vodka *whoosh*. Darkness moved and shivered all around as he stood and watched the flames, remembering the church and his night up on Swarth Coum. As he smiled, something in his brain flipped to famine.

He ran up to his room and opened another wrap and racked a few lines, inhaling, swallowing acrid snot. Feasting, feasting. He finished the first gram and opened another and pulled the carpets up and threw them out the window and cleaned the floors. Then he made a drugged-out trip into the nuclear glare of Homebase. Cruising the aisles, feeling bulletproof, laughing to himself, the whole jerk-off Fuck You of a cocaine high.

He got a taxi back with the tubs and brushes and sheets and began painting the floors and walls of his flat in brilliant and eggshell and glossy white. He painted over the montage of women's faces and placed white throws and bed sheets over everything and then he cut and shaved his hair off.

He went into the bathroom and smudged the lipsticked words across the mirror. Then he positioned his armchair in the centre of the room and sat there, feeling like he never wanted to sleep again.

He repeated it to himself until the word became a mantra, a phonological blur.

Like he'd had a fucking stroke:

I am an Asphyxiophiliac. I am an Asphyxiophiliac. I am an Asphyxiophiliac.
I am an Asphyxiophiliac. I am an Asphyxiophiliac. I am an Asphyxiophiliac.
I am an Asphyxiophiliac. I am an Asphyxiophiliac. I am an Asphyxiophiliac.
I am an Asphyxiophiliac. I am an Asphyxiophiliac. I am an Asphyxiophiliac.
I am an Asphyxiophiliac. I am an Asphyxiophiliac. I am an Asphyxiophiliac.
I am an Asphyxiophiliac. I am an Asphyxiophiliac. I am an Asphyxiophiliac.
I am an Asphyxiophiliac. I am an Asphyxiophiliac. I am an Asphyxiophiliac.
I am an Asphyxiophiliac. I am an Asphyxiophiliac. I am an Asphyxiophiliac.
I am an Asphyxiophiliac. I am an Asphyxiophiliac. I am an Asphyxiophiliac.
I am an Asphyxiophiliac. I am an Asphyxiophiliac. I am an Asphyxiophiliac.
I am an Asphyxiophiliac. I am an Asphyxiophiliac. I am an Asphyxiophiliac.
I am an Asphyxiophiliac. I am an Asphyxiophiliac. I am an Asphyxiophiliac.
I am an Asphyxiophiliac. I am an Asphyxiophiliac. I am an Asphyxiophiliac.
I am an Asphyxiophiliac. I am an Asphyxiophiliac. I am an Asphyxiophiliac.
I am an Asphyxiophiliac. I am an Asphyxiophiliac. I am an Asphyxiophiliac.
I am an Asphyxiophiliac. I am an Asphyxiophiliac. I am an Asphyxiophiliac.
I am an Asphyxiophiliac. I am an Asphyxiophiliac. I am an Asphyxiophiliac.
I am an Asphyxiophiliac. I am an Asphyxiophiliac. I am an Asphyxiophiliac.
I am an Asphyxiophiliac. I am an Asphyxiophiliac. I am an Asphyxiophiliac.
I am an Asphyxiophiliac. I am an Asphyxiophiliac. I am an Asphyxiophiliac.
I am an Asphyxiophiliac. I am an Asphyxiophiliac. I am an Asphyxiophiliac.
I am an Asphyxiophiliac. I am an Asphyxiophiliac. I am an Asphyxiophiliac.
I am an Asphyxiophiliac. I am an Asphyxiophiliac. I am an Asphyxiophiliac.

THE UNFAMILIAR TONES of his doorbell shocked him.

Jade took one look at him.

— Your beautiful hair?

Then at the flat.

— What the *fuck*?

Antony rubbed the suede of his freshly shorn head.

Jade punched him in the chest.

— What the fuck's *wrong* with you?

— Hit me again. Harder. Please.

She threw herself onto his bed.

— It's a new start, Jade.

Her blood-flushed, livid face.

— But you're a transvestite?

— It's not as simple as that.

— You gay?

— I think, he said. Think about your naked body every minute of every day.

She got off the bed and paced around the room, rubbing wetness from her cheeks.

— Then why?

— I'm starting to feel happy. I think I'm starting to like myself.

— You've never *liked* yourself?

He didn't see her move but she was all around him. The

smell of her hair, the pressure of her arms. He heard himself say it,

— I love you.

She took a step back. She blinked once, lips opened, nose flaring.

— I don't, she said. Don't know who you really are.

— That makes two of us. But I'm making a start.

She went over to the window, pointing at the racked-up lines.

— You twisted?

She barked a laugh, peering down into the yard outside.

He looked around the white room. The only things left were his mother's cremains, the address book, the black square of his laptop, and the framed photograph of him and Jade sitting in the centre of the mantelpiece.

And it was then that he noticed Jade's footprints across the floor. The cleat-marks of her trainers had made an upside-down question mark.

¿

A noose.

— Let's get away from this fucking flat, she said. It's freaking me out.

Neither of them moved.

— But I haven't got a stitch to wear.

— I'm really worried about you, she said.

— I'm sorry about my reaction to the whole university business. I know it's selfish, but I don't want to lose you.

She frowned distantly. She seemed to disappear for a second.

— We can only ever be friends.

He heard her voice and said,

— I've been telling you that all along.

HE OPENED HIS WINDOW. The cool air came to him as did the increasing noise from their bedroom. He felt hollow then, but he knew that soon everything would be all right, because he would climb down the drainpipe and pedal away on his bike, out past the estate and into the darkness of the country lanes where he would let go of the handlebars, his arms steeply outstretched like the wings of a dove, and the wind slowly stroking his hair would be the delicate long fingers of Cynthia Chester. A sense of calm would pass over him then, and he would be screaming *Wha-hooo* all the way, weaving along the back lanes down to the dovecote. There, he would remove the spare key from under the brick and let himself in. He would make a bed for himself in the creaking wicker chair and read his book, learning the Latin slanty words by torchlight.

Louder now. The shouting was getting much louder.

He climbed up onto the windowsill, rolled onto his stomach, and slowly slid out backwards. The drainpipe was just within reach.

He got a good foothold, and disappeared into the dark.

VIII

— Sorry to hear about your mother, Jack said.
— Thanks.
— Christmas.
— What about it?
— I know it's a couple of months away yet, but we were wondering.
— We?
— Your step-mum and me.
— . . .
— Would you like to come spend it here?
— You're joking?
He stared at his reflection in the mirror. Saw his mother's face.
— Antony?
— I'll think about it.

HE WALKED DOWN THE long winding driveway of dank woodland and found Jade's halls at the very bottom, an attractive three-storey Georgian villa with small leaded windows – it formed a semicircle around a perfectly tended lawn, dotted with enormous ochre acacias. And seeing her in those new surroundings, seeing that brain of hers being put to some use, he felt so entirely envious. He realized he'd let his own brain turn to mush and how much he missed being a student, the whole concentrated thrust of it.

She was lonely and tearful that first week and said she missed everyone, that Freshers' Week should have been called Fuckers' Week and that the place was full of posh Southern wankers. She even spoke about chucking the course in, but by the third week she'd made friends with a girl from Newcastle and they were going out a lot. The whole shared experience of being Northerners. Antony pictured the two young women surrounded by well-shod, twattish young men – panting, sweating, swarming.

ACCORDING TO HER clock it had just gone 9:30 and they were sat drinking G&Ts in her bedroom listening to tunes. They were meant to be catching the firework display at the Cathedral, but he knew they'd never make it out of her room that night. He'd begun to talk. For once, he'd started to open up.

— My mother was a dyke, he said flatly.

She leaned back and straightened her bra. He felt a stab of envy.

— She was gay. Big deal. So's my brother.
— Eh?
— John. Don't tell me you didn't?

She laughed and said,

— I take it you weren't happy about it, then?
— John's gay?
— Him and Moon, they're like *lovers*.
— It's more complicated than you think.
— I thought you of all people.
— Me of all people what?

She walked across the room and changed the CD. Their thoughts ping-pong'd along to the sound of Pulp. She leaned against her desk and he noticed how his eyes kept scrolling her figure, undressing her.

She folded her arms.

— It was the town I grew up in, he said. The way the adults looked at me. The hissing sound of *lezzer* behind my back. I wasn't even allowed to play with some of the kids, like the parents thought it was contagious. And of course they all thought I was gay. Bent by association.
— Sounds tough.
— Worst thing was not understanding it.
— Do you think that's why you're, you know?

There was a knocking on the bedroom door. Jade went into the corridor and he could hear her talking to another girl. He felt like he was going to burst. She came back in wearing a conspiratorial smile.

— I told her we'd see her in the bar later.

THEY SAT TOGETHER on her bed, facing the wall where an academic-year planner hung flecked with notes and coloured stars. She took his hand and ran her fingers along his knuckles. She opened her mouth, exhaling breezily,

— Out with it, then.

— It was all *wrong*, he said. I felt like a freak. Like you'd catch it from me. I'd walk down the street and I'd hear them whispering. Mother a pissed-up dyke and a bad-bastard father in prison. He'll not grow up right. That mother of his, the way she carries on. And Lou. Mother let that fat fucking dog . . .

He walked across the room and pressed his back against the wall.

— But what made you happy? Something must have made you happy?

— Dressing up, he said. The birds.

— The *birds*?

He told her about Eddie, about the dovecote.

He told her about the Blue Hour and poaching on the moors, and that no matter how bad things got, he could always find redemption in nature.

— I can't believe you've never talked about it before. How come there's this whole side to you that you never show?

— They were my real mum and dad, he said. Eddie and Val. I filled the gap Val's children had left. And the gap Eddie's son had left.

— Filling gaps?

He shrugged.

— Well, you've got to forget, Ant.

— I don't . . .

— No. I mean forget the person who doesn't remember this stuff.

— Forget remember?

She stood up, took a single step towards him.

— Come here.

He rubbed his eyes. Fireworks started whizzing and exploding in the city outside.

Jade moved forwards and touched him gently.

— Tell me. Please.

— I don't want to be a tranny, Jade. I don't want to be one

of those ugly fucking freaks hobbling around Canal Street with their stubble and bad wigs.

He hid his face in his hands.

Laughter echoed through his blood.

HE TRIED TO GIVE himself a quickie, fingers exploring the vessels and sinew of his neck. He found the arterial fork, the carotid sinus, and began to press, slowing the liquid pulse of life. Embraced by a flickering spark-light, he began to feel euphoric.

But then he heard a voice shouting down his veins,

— STOP.

The golden flowers faded, the high-speed clouds halted, he felt the cold white floor beneath his feet and the sparks ceased whizzing. It was like the stillness before the Blue Hour, the way the night seemed to dissolve before your eyes. Like she was touching his dreams again. Protecting him. Keeping him suspended. Leading him by hand into a land of confusion. Stop.

He pressed his head against the cool windowpane, watching children playing in the street outside, pedalling figure-of-eights on their bicycles, when the music of an ice-cream van made their heads turn in perfect synchronicity.

A solitary tear plopped onto the sill.

He began to leak.

HE FOUND HIMSELF WALKING into a firework shop on Oldham Street advertising skyrockets and sparklers at half-price – leftovers from Bonfire Night.

— What's the largest make you've got?

The man brought a box out from beneath the counter.

— Satellite Busters from Russia, he said in a put-on accent. He leaned towards Antony and whispered,

— Not strictly legal.

By the time Antony got to Canal Street it was starting to drizzle. He headed into Via Fossa and ordered a Guinness and wandered back into the churchy pews. There, sat in a booth, was Spooner, sans sad spectacles, with a bloke Antony was introduced to as Jeremy.

Straight people went to Canal Street all the time, but Antony was waiting for them to say it,

— Why you in a gay bar, Antony? You curious?

His new haircut didn't help.

They chatted and Antony noticed the booze had alleviated Spooner's spoonerisms. Antony called him by his real name,

— Another pint, Frank?

He got a fresh round in and smiled when Frank put his hand on Jeremy's thigh and didn't give a flying one. But then same-sex fondling was hardly new to him.

— I've wanted to mention this for a while now, Frank said.

I've secured a bit of funding for someone to conduct some research for six months.

— Go on.

— Into why the South Asian community aren't accessing the Centre.

— You mean Pakistani? You mean Muslim?

— I mean Muslim. You man enough?

— You're joking?

— Don't act so surprised. You're the only one at the Centre with any nouse.

Antony shook his head.

— Can you drive?

— Yeah.

— We can get you a car, then.

The three men looked at each other, smiling.

— But, Antony said.

— What?

— I want a new laptop.

— Comes with the job.

— And I want you to pay for me to do more signing lessons. Work hours.

Frank looked impressed.

— Consider it done. You can start after Christmas.

Antony raised his glass and decided that if he didn't leave soon he was going to start blabbing, get totally twatted, probably leave his bags somewhere and have to hand in his resignation on Monday with the sheer embarrassment of it all. Outside, the sunset city sky was bruised an orange-purple glow. How dramatic, he thought.

He popped into the dank New Union pub and pretended to pick up a few flyers.

He didn't see a single tranny.

MOONLIGHT FILLED the white room. When he closed his eyes, he saw the image of a woman's figure stood in the centre of the floor, floating, rotating slowly above the upside-down question mark. Twisting, retwisting.

Warm feelings flooded over him.

Did he want to be a woman? No. Though he imagined life would be so much better. No. He enjoyed being a man. No. He wanted to be normal. No. He wanted to be a girl. No. He wanted breasts, a clitoris, a vagina, a womb. No. To go back into remission, his monochrome masculine life. No. Date a woman, get married, settle down, have kids, only to have his wife catch him wearing her underwear. Maybe.

Empty nights waiting for her, feeling as if he was only half in this life. How his skin sang when she was with him. But most of the time – mostly it was as if he was impersonating her. A ventriloquist's dummy. When he dressed, she would start to hum the tune of him and suddenly the world became an interesting place.

Don't be like your mother.

— THANKS FOR RINGING ME.

    — What do you want? Jade asked.

    — That's nice. I was wondering what you're doing tomorrow?

    — Sorry. Just got back. Mum's in a proper stinker.

    — Want to escape tomorrow? Fancy a wee drive in the country?

    — You got it?

Antony looked at the Rover parked outside and smiled.

    — Yeah. It's *gorgeous*.

But driving away from the Centre that afternoon, he knew how much he'd miss the clients, the intimate intensity of the work, the loutish laughter.

He might even miss Derek.

    — Tops, she said. What colour?

    — Black. It's big and black.

    — She squealed.

    — And very shiny.

    — She moaned.

    — Powerful, shiny, fast.

    — Stop. Come rescue me NOW.

    — Can't. Been smoking.

    — Dopehead.

    — Why's Eileen cross?

    — You'll have to wait and see. No earlier than twelve, I need a fat lie in.

It was 1984 and he was crouched on his bedroom floor, thighs pressed against his chest, swaying gently as he prayed in that dread-filled way for them to stop, trying to remember a time when things were different, but there never was such a time. He peered through the crack in the curtains: Lou, storming off up the garden path in the pre-dawn light. Behind him, out of view, marched the rest of the streets on the estate.

He saw two tiny red dots: the sulphur head of a match being struck and the end of the cigarette glowing. Lou turned the engine over and drove away at speed.

He heard his mother descending the stairs. He imagined her meaty fingers passing through thick damp hair; purple bunions protruding like baby beetroot from the insides of her milk-white feet; spider-hairy toes curled up against the cold. There was a chattering of kitchen sounds: steel against steel, pot against pan, bowl clunking against the wood of the tabletop. He heard the bubble of a sob. Heard Motown playing.

He wanted to go down there, to comfort her. Just the two of them again.

It was all he ever wanted.

THEY SMILED PLAYFULLY AT the kissing-gates. Clarty-arsed sheep watched them in disgust, the ineptly dressed hikers in fleece hats, trainers and trendy cagoules, trundling along the causey path between the Hushings and Hurstwood Reservoir.

Antony read aloud from his guidebook. He told her about how exploiters had burrowed wounds deep into the tops of the moors, draining and gathering waters like acid bile, then spewing back the clay and soil to reveal the lime, leaving these be-grassed spoil heaps in their wake. The Hushings.

Jade laughed.

— I feel like we've entered Teletubby Land.

She made him shut the guidebook and began chattering cheerily about university and her new friends – most of whom, Antony noted, were male. Again this sense she was gliding away from him into a new world that he only heard about, and to which he would never belong, a sense she was making a retreat so measured, so fine, that he wouldn't register the moment she released him back into his paused life.

They were passing a solitary copse of trees that looked like the X-rays of aged lungs when Antony stumbled over a mound of mat grass, disturbing a red grouse.

Fat, barely flying bird, its cry made them jump.

— It's probably your hair that did it, Antony said.

— Thanks.

— Scaring the wildlife. No wonder your mum freaked.

Jade tucked a loose strand of fringe hair under her hat.

— Should come with a health warning, he said.

— Funny-ha-ha.

— Why pink?

— I think you'll find it's Persian Rose, actually.

HALFWAY up the hill they stopped to admire the view: the reservoir reflected the caesium-blue sky and in the distance Coal Clough wind farm resembled an army of eerie white robots, arms spinning headlong. Jade pointed out the black speck of his Rover in the car park.

Within an hour they reached the high watershed: a thin post marking the border between Lancashire and Yorkshire. On Antony's map it looked like Morse code, and he imagined packhorses straining up there along the dash-dot-dash, sweating beneath their burden of loom and spinning jenny for the neighbouring mills.

— The sky up here's so enormous, Jade said.

He kept waiting for the perfect moment to capture it all: the low sun, its wintry orange sharpness lighting Jade's smile in 35mm, but she kept shying away from the camera.

A sudden, rude howling of wind made tears plop down her face.

— Fancy some scran?

— Aye, she said. I'm proper freezing.

They began heading the short distance to a stony outcrop, the Gorple Stones, when Jade came to a sudden halt and hugged herself.

— You didn't tell me we'd be wading through bogs.

— It's fine, he said. Howay man.

The singsong of his childhood accent, surprising him.

— But my feet, she said. They're blocks of ice.

She gave him an imploring look and so he piggybacked her

247

over to the boulders, their belly laughs piercing the thick moor air.

Antony emptied his bag and laid it on the ground and they leaned against the massive, humanoid rocks, looking out over the landscape.

He opened the flask and poured the coffee and took the Clingfilm off the cheese-and-pickle butties.

— Sorry they're squashed.

— Ne'er mind. By the way, Eileen wants to know if you're coming next week.

— Eh?

— I'll understand if you don't want to come. Christmas like.

That pitiful tone. A hundred peripheral thoughts jostled in his skull.

He took a deep breath and said,

— I'm off to Spain.

— What, to see your dad?

— See Jack, yes.

She opened her mouth.

— I'm nervous about seeing him, he said. I'm nervous about meeting my half-brother and step-mum. Stupid, isn't it?

She smiled and he said,

— It'll be the first Christmas I've ever spent with him.

She snuggled into his arm and squeezed.

He scanned the barium clouds above, thinking of home and his night on Swarth Coum, the day he'd met Jack for the first time.

He was suddenly overwhelmed by the fact he had a father.

THEY FINISHED EATING and drinking in silence and packed the rucksack up. Jade said she didn't want to walk any further, so they made their way back down the valley, stopping halfway to catch their breaths, sitting on a large rock beside a beck in spate with snowmelt.

— I never told you, he said. I was engaged to Rebecca.

Jade removed her hat. The blueness of her eyes held the sky, contrasting so vibrantly against the deep pink of her hair.

— Rebecca, he said. Must be some kind of record.

He looked away. He didn't want to read Jade's expression.

— Nine fucking days. I don't think she ever loved me. But there was something about her, she made me so ... She always kept me at arm's length, which made me even more . . .

He tapped the side of his head and said,

— Desperate.

— So why'd you propose to her?

— I didn't want to lose her.

— She finished with you because you're a tranny.

It wasn't a question.

— You hid it from her?

He exhaled heavily, nodded.

— You'll find someone, you know, who doesn't mind. Who's supportive. You've just got to stop lying. There's nothing less attractive than a liar.

— Is that you being subtle, then?

She finger-combed her hair and sighed.

— We can only ever be friends, Ant. You *know* that.

— You've no idea how much that means to me.

— Anyway, I think there's only room for one woman in your life right now.

He clambered to his feet.

— Since when did you get to be so fucking smart?

— Seeing you talking to Rebecca that night, it made me realize.

— What?

— Help me.

He pulled her up. She brushed her backside as they faced each other.

— I'm not sure you'll want to hear this.

— What?

249

— I think you're attracted to them.

He shrugged.

— Complete bitches, she said.

Her breath appeared to fall from her mouth. She put a fist to her chest and her eyes said I'm sorry. He smiled a smile that said you're right.

HE DREAMT IN SIGN LANGUAGE and woke up crying. He was by his mother's side at her deathbed and he was the last thing she saw in this life. He was trying to tell her something but for some reason he couldn't speak, and so he had to fingerspell the words for her: I'm sorry. The dream was so intense he could actually feel it in his organs, but when he woke properly and saw his white room and rubbed the nap of his head, he felt like a mental patient; that he'd been sectioned for years and his life in Manchester with Rebecca and Jade was just a tripped-out, medicated nightmare. The white room became a screen upon which this other life was projected.

He couldn't remember the last time he'd wept, and now he was doing it in his sleep. The stark, solid, 3D reality hit him: he was truly alone. The physical sensation dissipated, but the emotional imprint lasted a few minutes longer.

He stared at the upside-down question mark of footprints on his floor.

Wondering what would be waiting for him at the other end.

IX

HE SAW IT AS a huge metal cigar tearing through the dark, hurtling through the sky above England, France and finally Spain where Jack would be waiting for him at the airport. He knocked back the whisky and lined the plastic cup up next to the others.

An old woman across the aisle kept glancing over at him and smiling; he made the mistake of smiling back.

— I'm onto my second, love. I hate flying too.

The old woman's voice: frayed, hoary, two-packs-a-day. She raised her almost empty beaker for Antony to see.

— I quite like flying, he said.

— Oooh, it puts the willies up me. I mean all of this weight in the clouds?

Antony leaned over into the aisle, searching for a stewardess, the plastic-feeling euros sweaty in his hand. The old lady went on to tell Antony how many children, grandchildren and great-grandchildren she had, and that she'd been coming to the same resort for nearly thirty-odd years with her two friends here. Antony looked at the elderly couple next to her, sleeping, open-mouthed, the little rectangular peel-off containers in their laps.

The old lady added that it was the four of them last year, but her husband had died two months ago.

— It'll be hard this year without him, she said.

— I'm sorry.

— Yes, love, so am I.

Antony quickly pulled his Discman out, slipped the headphones on, and closed his eyes.

IT HIT HIM HARD: Jack had a whole life where Antony didn't even figure, and he couldn't help thinking about that journey home from the prison and the fight he'd had with his mother after. It was his eleventh birthday and he'd just met his father for the first time and she would never let him forget it. She was meant to be on the late shift, and he knew what her being home meant. He tested her with one or two comments; she began to bite. The tension was like a magnet; he felt coiled, tight.

He wanted her to look at him, to notice the buzz inside of him.

— So, he said. You never told us he wanted to marry you.

Dead silence and a stone-cold stare.

— He said he came back when I were four.

She pig-snorted down her nose.

— Said he didn't know I were born.

— Shite and like.

— Said he came back when I were four and asked you to marry him and you told him to fuck off.

She raised a glass to her lips and took big mouthfuls, looking out of the window.

— I know about copulation, he said. I know about fucking.

Her tongue-pink mouth as she laughed.

— I'm not daft.

— I'm gonna fettle you, laddo.

They sat in the bruised silence. The animosity was thick, but he felt buoyed up by it, because he had something now, something she could never take away. The crow's feet around Jack's sloe-berry eyes when he smiled – that's what made Antony real. The lined contours of Jack's life, formulating

256

something that felt like home. She could rain down whatever words she wanted to now – he liked his father and his father liked him.

So fuck you.

— I bet you wish you'd never had me?

The curl of her lip, eyes glowering.

— Yes, she said.

Just like that. A hard-nosed *yes*.

And she was there in a shot, a bulky mass above him. He curled his fist into a hard rock and struck her breast. She grabbed herself with a gasp as he leapt off the settee.

It was happening again.

He edged backwards towards the door.

— You little BASTARD.

The dull sting of his brain hitting the inside of his skull, the pressure and blackness about the eyes. He got up, gripping onto the back of the chair. He'd said everything else and so barked it out, the one thing he hadn't said,

— FUCKING LESBIAN.

The shocking sound of it. The times he'd heard it in whispers and shouts, written all over the snide faces of the town.

— Fuck you.

All those faces were her.

— Fuck you.

Backing out of there, their eyes locked.

— FUCK.

She felt along the edge of the fireplace.

— YOU.

She was wielding the poker by her side. He charged at it, trying to unpeel her fingers from the handle. The nails on her free hand dug into his scalp and she was dragging him by his hair into the kitchen, feet sliding across the lino, down the steps and into the backyard. She was lifting him off the ground, making grunting animal sounds.

He knew where he was going.

— No-no-no-no-no . . .

Kicking and wailing, flinging his arms out wide.

— Pleasepleasepleasepleasepleaseplease . . .

But she was so fucking strong.

The coalhouse door opened. He felt her hands tighten around his neck. Manky colours smudged and flared in his head, and at that moment he didn't care whether he lived or died. At eleven years of age, he'd simply had enough.

He fell into the cold, slippery darkness.

— And you can go live with your bastard father when he gets out.

Her footsteps, gone.

But the door remained opened.

Mother, fading.

HE TOOK A SEAT beneath the shade of a large tatty-looking cycad, staring at his hands, lulled by the soft vibrato of cicadas. It felt wrong somehow, the heat in the wintertime, and the sun was a dream that smothered him. He rubbed the sweat from his temples and sighed heavily, intimidated by the thoughts in his head.

The toilet door clicked open and Jack stepped out.

He sat on the bench opposite Antony and began stroking the mangy-looking cat. The cat's unblinking eyes, two sable scintillas of pupil set into emerald discs, observed Antony with feline loathing. Jack's thick sun-dark forearms flexed, making the blue-smudge of a tattoo twitch.

He could sense his father grappling with something, the wings of words trapped in his mouth, and Antony suddenly felt like an intruder.

— So what do you think?

Jack smiled, showing his perfectly white capped teeth, nodding haughtily towards the restaurant.

It was such a cliché, the retired gangster in Spain with the British bar pandering to the safe monoculture of the ex-pat community and their longings for fish and chips and tepid pints of John Smiths.

— Great spot, Antony said. Love the harbour.

The cat's tail whip-flickered.

— Been a good earner this season, Jack said. Think I'll open throughout the winter next year. Carla needs a break, though. She's a good little worker.

Carla, Antony's sleek-haired, doe-eyed stepmother. Catalan, sexy, and four years younger than Antony. He spent last night trying not to look at her.

— No doubt Daniel will be up early tomorrow, wanting his presents.

Antony nodded.

— He hasn't stopped talking about you.

— Wish I could understand him.

— He understands more than he can speak.

— Wish I'd made an effort to learn a bit.

Antony recalled the awkwardness at the airport as they shook hands like complete strangers. The whole anticlimax of it.

Jack stood.

— There's something I want to show you.

Jack tooled the Beemer along winding pot-holed roads, and soon the sienna-coloured stuccoed streets dwindled into orchards, cypresses and orange groves. Antony hated himself for wanting to make a good impression, like his father was interviewing him for the position of Son. But when his father started talking about one of the young waitresses he was fucking, Antony felt the comedown. The intimate details were in no way intimate, and intimacy was exactly what he wanted. Antony half-listened, shivering in the icy blast of the aircon as they made their way up into the mountains.

Jack pointed through the windscreen. Above the tall pine trees, Antony could make out the pinkish walls of a monastery and an enormous stone cross.

— El Picot, Jack said solemnly. Sanctuary of Sant Salvador.

They pulled into the car park and stepped out into the heat.

Antony followed Jack towards the large terrace wall, walking behind him, observing.

— It still had a monk when I first got here, Jack said. Last one on the island.

The blue of the enamel sky and sea.

I'd use oils, Antony thought. Or gouache. Bondi blue. Cornflower.

His father beckoned him to the rail.

— That's Cap de Formento. That over there, that's Cabrera.

The tangerine Serra Mountains flickering in a haze.

— And that peak in the distance, that's the Castell de Sanueri. An old Arab fortress. Moorish.

Antony thinking who is this talking?

Jack hooked his thumb over his shoulder.

— And the town we came through, Felinitx, that's where Christopher Columbus was born.

Jack's accent: a weird hybrid of cockney smeared with a Catalan tilt.

— Come on.

Jack led them into the cool, echoing chambers of the monastery, between salmon alabaster walls lit in a soupy candlelight.

Antony followed the large man around the womb-like space, hoping he would find the answer in the next two days, the way to unbind those words trapped in Jack's mouth.

HE WOKE TO FIND his own face staring back at him. Daniel's small, bony finger prodded his ribs again, his breath chocolaty sweet.

— Papa Noel, he enthused. Papa Noel.

Antony rubbed his eyes. The bed was claggy with sweat. He got up and followed his brother into the living room. Jack, his hair sticking on end, was struggling with a camcorder, wearing nothing but his boxer shorts.

A singsong voice came from behind him,

— Merry Christmas, Antony.

Carla, sitting on the settee, watching TV with the sound turned low. She smiled warmly, running fingers through her hair.

— Buenos, err . . .

Carla laughed.

— Bon Nadal, she said.

— Bon Nadal, Antony repeated. Bon Nadal.

Jack shook his head and grunted at the tripod.

— Right. Got the twat.

The three adults stared at each other.

And so it began.

Antony wished he could disappear, his face aching dully with a faux-smile as he watched his father and Daniel together: unwrapping Daniel's presents; Daniel curling his arms around

Jack's legs; Daniel's wilful pouting and carefree laughter; Jack sweeping the small boy into his arms, kissing and embracing him so unselfconsciously.

It wasn't that he didn't want Daniel to have Jack's love – it was just seeing the life he'd always wanted being played out in front of him like that. All of it captured on VHS, except for Antony's heart burning in his chest.

He moved slowly out of the house and walked through the garden towards a lone olive tree. The way the morning sunshine lit the garden – he felt like a 2D figure in a garish trompe-l'œil painting.

Wishing he hadn't come.

Wishing he'd stayed at home.

YELLOW SLABS OF MEDITERRANEAN light warmed the kitchen's parquet floor as he stood chatting to Carla. She wore a long flowery blue dress, open at the neck, revealing a satin-sheened décolletage and ample cleavage. Antony watched her chopping garlic, putting her weight behind a pestle as she ground almonds in a shiny brass mortar. Sexy little groans and snorts, heavy breasts swaying, soft mouth saying such soft things, those full lips designed for sucking.

Again, he wondered what the hell she was doing with his father, the nearly sixty-year-old man tinkering with the generator in the backyard and swearing loudly.

It was, he realized, like his father fucking Jade.

Carla moved quickly about the kitchen, draining some bread, pouring the almonds and garlic into a blender, adding oil. Then she tipped the mixture into a tureen of grapes and searched the shelves for something, speaking her fast, broken English while Antony struggled with his eyes, envying her effortless, sultry dark beauty.

If he closed his eyes he'd see himself wearing Carla's dress, and the idea of wearing her made him cross his legs.

She put her hands on her hips and sighed, waking him from the dream of her.

— OK.

He followed her into the dining room and took a seat at the

large oak table and said a thank you as she served the gazpacho. She poured four bowls and shouted something fierce in Catalan. Daniel remained on the floor, playing with one of his presents. She took a seat and tutted, gesturing wildly.

— Eat eat.

His father appeared, wiping oil-fingered hands on a tea towel. In a shot, Daniel was at the table and suddenly it was the four of them. Antony sneaked another peek at Carla's cleavage and then stared down into the bowl: orbs of grapes covered in white sauce. He swallowed hard, wishing someone would speak.

Jack, Carla, Daniel — they supped and slurped hungrily.

DANIEL PUSHED his bowl away and produced a toy figure, making it dance while singing loudly. Jack growled at him and Carla lifted a piece of fruit from the bowl. She held it out in front of Daniel's wide, umber eyes.

— Mandarina, she said. Yum-yum. Mandarina.

She peeled it in front of him and then offered him a piece, taking a segment for herself and putting it in her mouth, sucking her fingers.

— Man-da-rina, she repeated.

Antony realized he was staring at her.

— He's a fussy eater, Jack said. A real pain, aren't you, son?

— I ate like a horse as a kid, Antony said.

Daniel smiled a gap-filled smile, offering Antony a part-chewed segment.

— Mandarina, Daniel said. Yum-yum.

— Got my arse tanned if I left food on my plate, Antony said snidely.

Carla stood up to clear the plates; Jack stared mutely at his callused hands.

SKITTISH TINY LIZARDS scattered between the frangipani and furry euphorbia that seemed to be jostling for space along the garden's high walls.

— I'm pulling them out to make room for geraniums, Jack said.

Antony moved away again; Jack followed.

Jack hadn't asked are you OK?

Jack hadn't asked how are things back home?

Not even a cursory are you happy?

Thanks again for the present, Antony said, fingering the Zippo lighter.

The two men walked a wide arc to avoid the rotating lawn sprinklers, and headed towards the large kidney-shaped swimming pool in silence.

HE STEPPED OUT of the bar and onto the quiet esplanade. The Christmas Day sun was beginning to sink behind the mountains and the small harbour was a swathe of twisted, twinkling lights. Painted fishing boats bobbed in front of the waterfront bars filled with ex-pat families enfolded in communal, festive cheer.

There had been a few muzzy looks as he'd sat beside Carla and Daniel. Carla, Jack, Antony – they all knew why: Antony and Carla looked like a couple, like a young family together.

Grandfather Jack.

Antony sat on the harbour wall, picturing Kenneth and Julia and Kerry in Christleton. He thought about Jade and what she'd said about Rebecca at the Hushings. Then he reminded himself how desperate Eddie was for him and Jack to have a reunion, to have some kind of relationship.

He looked over towards the bar where his father stood watching him, smoking.

They nodded at each other.

HIS LUNGS TIGHTENED AS he hit the cold water. Gasping, he pedalled water as Jack clung onto the side of the swimming pool, coughing with laughter.

Antony's jaw chattered.

— It's fucking freezing.

His father's long, sonorous laugh, making Antony feel so alive.

— Just try to relax.

The light came on at the back of the house and Carla appeared, walking towards them with drinks on a tray. Antony cuffed a hand over his balls as Carla looked down at the two men, shaking her head. She sat on the sun-lounger and lit a cigarette.

Jack had driven, trying to keep the Beemer in the middle of the road at a lethargic ten miles per hour. He whooped when he got out of the car and ran towards the swimming pool, shedding his clothes.

Jack twisted onto his back, pointing up.

— Look.

The star-mad Spanish sky. Antony recognized the double-U of Cassiopeia.

He tipped his head under. Water silenced the night.

RESTLESS, feeling effervescent, thinking about his father a few feet away behind the wall. It's all he ever wanted as a child – the close, reassuring presence of Jack in the next room.

Not the sound of a girl crying. Not the wet sounds of Mother and Lou.

He pictured his father blinking up at the ceiling when he heard Carla's voice.

A growl. A distinct,

— Como?

DANIEL WOKE HIM by shoving Buzz Lightyear's hand into his mouth. He put his face up to Antony's, his breath warm and sweet as he whispered earnestly, nodding his head. The boy's unconditional love, his carefree openness towards Antony – it was overwhelming. Antony lifted the boy from the bed and they walked out onto the warm veranda holding hands.

He never expected to stay more than three days. Booking the flight, he imagined probably leaving earlier than that, that things would be far more difficult than they were. But when he woke up that morning he felt so at ease.

Daniel played with Buzz, making his own *Toy Story* sound effects. Yawning, Antony sat down with his back against the wall and rubbed his face.

Daniel sidled close to him, twisting his legs.

— Are you my brother?

A coy but perfect English.

— Yes, Antony said. I am. I'm your brother.

Daniel sat on Antony's lap, resting a sleepy head against his shoulder.

Jack and Carla watching them from the garden, smiling.

LIT BY THE INTERMITTENT glare of the fairy lights that hung incongruously in the palm tree, the two men sat beside each other at the back of the garden. They'd been drinking for a few hours now, and Antony felt woozy and confused.

— Come stay for longer next time, Jack said.

— Yeah.

— You could have stayed longer. We could've gone to a bullfight.

— I've things to do. My new job and that.

Jack offered him a cigarette and lit it. Antony exhaled, smoke sailing upwards.

He got a waft of Jack's whiskey: an earthy bouquet. He watched how Jack drank, how he took a sip into his mouth and held it there, and when he swallowed it was with a slightly pained look. Finally, he'd drag a thumb across his thick tache and sigh.

— I'm proud of you, Jack said. Of how you turned out.

The words in Antony's head: Dad, I'm a transvestite.

— You ever fancy a change, a break, there's a job here at the restaurant.

— Cheers.

— I've been thinking of getting a new manager. Carla needs a rest from it all.

— Right.

— So what happened to you and Rebecca, then?

— There was another woman in my life.

— Good lad. Play the field.

They were so alike but so completely different: Antony, raised by his mother and Lou to hate men, to see them as pathetic, weak, as wholly unreliable – the absent, errant Jack being conclusive proof of this; and there was Jack, a real man's man, the small-time gangster, the ex-con who bragged about cheating on his beautiful young wife.

Jack took his wallet from his breast pocket and pulled out a small photograph.

— Who's that, then?

Antony saw himself in the black-and-white, sat on a horse as a teenager.

— I can't remember this being taken, he said.

Jack belly-laughed, making the ice in his glass tinkle.

— It's your grandfather. He was small, like you. Every time I look at you, I see him. It's weird. You're his pot model.

— Pot-what?

— His twin.

Antony passed the photograph back and said,

— I see there are no photos of me in the house.

IT WAS THE FIRST TIME Antony had heard any of this and he wasn't too sure he wanted to know. Jack, speaking nostalgically about his time inside, about his enhanced rep and incumbent dealers, about form and doing brown in his prison cell.

Antony stared down into his drink.

— Heroin, it's like you're trapped inside your body and you want to escape. There I was, locked inside the cell and inside my own head. Ha.

Farm dogs barked and goat-bells clunked somewhere in the darkness.

— No tabs, Jack said. No phone cards. None of that *Porridge* bullshit.

Antony was struggling to concentrate.

— There's always problems when a cellmate's in for a lesser sentence. They become gate-happy. The fucker constantly blabs on about when he's getting out and what he plans to do, blah-this and blah-that. I guess I just snapped.

And there was Antony at home as a child, imaging his father missing him.

— Stop it. Please.

—What?

— I'm not interested in you doing some poor cunt in. And I'm certainly not interested in you fucking some waitress up the arse and making her cry. You have any idea how lucky you are to have Carla?

— Keep your voice down.

— I'm *not* interested. I never will be.

Jack stood up slowly with a groan.

— It's lucky I had Eddie and Val, Antony said.

He watched Jack clench and unclench his fists.

— Do you know, Antony said, what I used to tell people?

Jack took a step towards him.

— I used to tell people that you were dead.

— Is there something you want to say?

— Meaning?

— Meaning is there something you want to ask me?

Jack's looming presence was intimidating. Antony got to his feet, telling himself: it's my father. Adrenalin turned his skin cold.

— Yeah, I've loads of questions.

Jack brushed his hair back from his face, features static.

— It's your fault I can't connect with anyone. It's your fault Mam became an alcoholic. And I don't know why I . . .

— Antony.

— Why I love you. Because I don't *want* to love you. I want to keep on hating you because you won't tell me who I am.

272

Jack's face appeared in sudden focus: a wild gleam in his eye.

— What?

— I don't even know where I come from. How I came about. I feel like I'm stuck. Suspended. I want you to tell me.

— What?

— The truth. Now that she's gone. The story of *me*.

Jack leaned against the wall and ran his hands over his hair. It was hard to tell what his expression was in that flickering light, but Antony could feel the gravity of his father's mood.

— I want to see you as something different, Antony said.

— Different from what?

— A coward. I see you as a fucking coward.

— She wanted a baby, Jack said. Without the man.

The words released.

— What?

— She knew, early on. That she was, you know.

— Say it.

— Gay. That she was gay.

Antony put his face in his hands.

— She wanted a kid, Jack said. That's all there is to it.

— How could you *do* that?

Jack turned away for a second. Antony said,

— Every man's fantasy, eh? Fucking a dyke.

— She never wanted me involved.

— You expect me to believe that?

— I didn't . . .

— She *wanted* me?

— Yeah. She did.

Antony pointed at him.

— How come she hated *you* so much, then?

Jack shrugged.

— Christmases, birthdays, did you never think about me?

— Course I did, Jack said.

— And all that stuff you told me when I saw you in prison.
— What stuff?
— About asking her to marry you.
— Antony.
— Do you not understand? I've no idea who I am.
— Your mother loved you.
— Bollocks.
— She was ill.
— Fuck that.
— I'd've been no father.
— You're right there.

Jack moved towards him and Antony flinched, cowered, but Jack's arms sucked him in. The tight, massive pressure of Jack hugging, hugging. Antony's face pressed against his father's chest. The two men felt each other's warmth for the very first time, but then they were looking into each other's eyes.

The smell of his father's breath in his face.

Jack turned and walked towards the house. Antony lifted a hand.

— Wait.

Jack climbed the steps onto the veranda and disappeared inside.

THE HOUSE WAS SILENT. He hadn't heard a single noise for minutes now, but the pain was too much – he desperately needed to piss. He got up and walked into the bathroom and relieved himself while looking at his face in the mirror, imagining Jack having to stoop.

He went into the living room. The TV was off and the front door was closed. The clock said it had just gone midday. He went into the garden and saw Carla stretched on a lilo in the swimming pool, wearing a black bikini and sunglasses.

He walked towards her.

— Morning, Carla.

Nothing.

— Holá?

The lilo shifted slightly, her hand stroking the water. Then he heard the scratch of music coming from her headphones.

He looked behind him. Jack's Beemer wasn't in the driveway.

He watched her floating there, his throat tightening in the glare of her beauty. There was something so deeply sexy about her body. He imagined licking the sharp ridge of her hip bones, licking circles around the tiny brown oyster of her bellybutton, kissing the skin beneath her breasts, sliding his tongue between the velvety folds of her labia, making her gasp.

He went back into the house and locked the bathroom door behind him. He took off his clothes and got into the shower. He could almost taste her breath, the yum of her full lips. He came so hard and so quickly he yelped with surprise.

SHE STOOD in her bedroom doorway brushing her hair.

— Jack told me say goodbye.

Just like water, he thought. The path of least resistance.

— But I'm due at the airport.

She flicked her hair over her shoulder. The soft smell of almonds, frangipani.

She placed a warm hand on his forearm

— I'll talking you.

— Talking?

— Ai ai. Come.

THEY DROVE past golf greens and cubist mansions, past shopping centres gleaming between the parasols of palms. He imagined himself with an easel and paints by the side of the road. How he'd capture the chiaroscuro effect of shadow with charcoal and an eraser's edge.

— Jack is Jack, she said. Does what he wants. You love him or don't. I know who he is. He told me you say you love him.

Antony nodded. In the distance, he could see the fortified walls of El Picot and remembered its cool, echoing alabaster chambers. He wondered where Jack was.

— But you want that be different, no?

— Sorry?

— You want things be different?

— Yes.

— Good. Jack, he just don't know how to show it.

They drove past pueblos and villa projects under construction, and he pictured himself wandering the fields like Van Gogh.

— I want baby, she said. Little sister, brother. For Daniel.

She paused.

— For you.

Happy laughter, happy words, her soft eyes creasing.

— Jack say no, but I know him. I stop the pill. Not tell.

She put a finger to her lips and they both laughed.

She dropped the Citroën into third for a bend, her knee lifting her skirt a fraction.

Antony saw her underskirt, its red lace edging.

She slapped his arm.

— I see you, naughty boy. Looking up Mummy's dress.

She winked playfully.

— Now be good boy and get Mummy's purse.

He looked around for her handbag. Daniel was awake on the back seat, tired eyes staring at him, blinking.

— Mummy need her cigarette.

X

JOYFUL

LONELINESS. It had shattered and bruised his life, but here he was choosing to spend New Year's Eve at home alone. When he got back from Spain and switched his mobile on, it had merrily buzzed away for a couple of minutes with messages. One from his father, or perhaps Carla, wishing him *Felic any Nou!* Two texts from Hattie, wishing him Merry Christmas, and one asking if he was OK. One, even, from John, inviting him out for drinks sometime. And a text from Jade about New Year – John was deejaying and did he want to go clubbing again, and, erm, could he score some pills?

Then the six voicemails from Hattie.

EXCITEMENT. He stood at the window waiting, eyeing the yard below, wondering who'd taken it upon themselves to remove the charred remains. Then he spotted the Argos van turning into the street and ran downstairs to give them a hand. He spent the rest of the day with a screwdriver and Allen key, assembling the flat-pack furniture, cursing the obtuse diagrams and his own stupidity. Furniture assembled, new wide-screen TV mounted, he stood back and looked upon his new home-slash-office with satisfaction, feeling like a *real* man. He was in melamine, mahogany-effect heaven. He shaved his hair with his new WAHL kit, then sat in the black leatherette chair and turned the TV up loud, spinning himself in dizzying circles, feeling the raw vibrancy of life again.

FALTERING. Frank spelled out exactly what Antony needed to do and gave him an initial list of contacts, including the imam at the local mosque and the Asian Disability Network.

He heard Derek in the corridor, laughing his infectious staccato laugh.

The gravity of the project suddenly hit him.

— And I'd like you to fill this in every day: Movements Chart.

— Two solids this morning and a wet fart at lunch?

— I know, it's ridiculous, but it's for the funders and Head Office, so make sure you fill it in properly.

— A-huh.

— You OK?

— Bit nervous, I guess.

Frank laid an avuncular hand on his shoulder.

— You'll do just fine. I have every confidence. Here.

He handed him a sheet of paper.

— Signing classes. BSL 2. Wednesday afternoons.

— If you weren't such a bender, I'd give you a big sloppy kiss.

— I'll take that as a compliment.

— You've no idea how much this means to me. I just hope I don't fuck up.

— It's my job to see to it that you don't. We'll have a review every Friday until you're settled. Now get cracking.

TENTATIVE. He didn't know whether he'd done the right thing by Kenneth over the past few months, but Kenneth appeared to be more than happy. In fact, he seemed peculiarly fulfilled. He'd familiarized himself with the unit and was picking up people's names – because (as Antony pointed out), the staff were using his aides-memoires properly – and he'd been to Julia's house for the first time and met Kerry. Though he still asked for Lizzie. Still listened for her footsteps. Still sniffed the air for her perfume.

But Antony was convinced that Kenneth had worked it out: Lizzie's screaming face (of anger) and the baby (Kerry's difficult breech birth), that they were two separate events, fused by his amnesia somehow.

He just hoped Kenneth learned to Save As instead of Delete.

The last time Antony saw him, Kenneth said,

— Lizzie hates me, doesn't she?

Antony asked him what he did yesterday.

BORED BORED BORED. Yes, the month had been a lonely month, though not entirely miserable because of that. His own company seemed more than pleasant, for once, but he knew he was missing something. When he focused on his eyes in the bathroom mirror, the final lipsticked word remained blurred but distinct. He tried to invoke its meaning—JOYful. JOYful. JoyFUL. But all he felt was stupid. He rubbed it off the mirror and felt the void of her and worried she'd left forever, for she was a spotlight illuminating his life, and his life had started slipping back into shade. Later, he was lying in bed with his eyes closed, jumping between the scenes of eyelid films. Thinking of his mother, the vision of her lying unconscious on the kitchen floor insinuated itself. How he'd always listen to make sure she was breathing and he'd hear that sound inside her: something breaking, something drowning. Thinking of his father, he saw himself in the black-and-white photograph, sitting on a horse as a teenager, and he could almost feel his double helices stringing back in time. Slowly adjusting to the reality of the here and now, he realized he was in his flat in Manchester with his mother in the room next door, resting in her white plastic box.

HATTIE OPENED THE DOOR and blinked at him in the half-light.

— What you doing here?

She ran her hands through sleep-jumbled hair.

— Sorry. Come on in, son.

He stepped into the warm, sleepy fug of the house, and followed her along the corridor, past the room where he'd last seen his mother alive.

Hattie hit the light in the kitchen and stared at the clock on the wall. She rubbed her eyes and turned a small radio on and ran water into the sink. The kitchen smelled of overfilled bin bags.

He'd driven all night; it felt as if the walls were moving.

She spoke to him with her back turned,

— I thought you weren't talking to me.

— How come?

— I've been trying to phone you over Christmas. Loads.

— I went to Spain for a few days.

She turned to him with an inflamed look on her face; his presence suddenly appeared to make sense to her.

— How *is* Jack?

A serrated edge to her voice.

— Same as ever, he said.

She finished cleaning the pots and set the table. She did it in an almost chirpy way, trying to lighten the atmosphere. The radio spoke about fishing quotas while they ate cereal and drank coffee. The morning began opening up outside, imbuing the kitchen with wan light.

— So how was it at your brother's place?

She laughed.

— A bloody mistake, that's what. My niece is going through that teenage monster stage. The whole two weeks it was all me me me. I dread to think what she'll be like in a few years.

She blew onto her coffee. The radio spoke about dog fouling.

— My brother's a total oddball. Has his moments though. You grow up in Meva, chances are you'll be a bit of a nutter.

Antony yawned heavily, bringing tears to his eyes.

— You suit your hair like that, she said.

— Cheers. I have that Fonz moment every morning.

He held an invisible comb to his head and then threw his arms out.

— Heyyyyyy. Every morning, perfect hair.

— You laugh just like your mother.

Disarmed, he rubbed his lips and swallowed drily.

Cornish Pirates, the radio said. Versus Plymouth Albion.

— I'd love to shave all of mine off.

— Really?

— No. But women get to a certain age and their hair turns against them.

Hypnotized by a sudden, crushing bout of fatigue, Antony stared vacantly around the kitchen. He rubbed his eyes and saw that closed bedroom door in his head.

— I know, she said. I know what you're looking for.

He focused on Hattie's face, the hard look there.

— Well there *ain't* any.

She went over to the sink, looking into the garden outside.

— But don't think it hasn't crossed my mind.

Antony tried to rewind the last few moments, looking for

empty bottles on the side. That's when he noticed the photograph on the fridge: Hattie and his mother; the drink in Hattie's hand; that look in his mother's eyes and her smile: a chimera of times gone.

He walked over to Hattie, placing a hand between her warm shoulder blades.

THEY WALKED down the steep, winding Polkirt Hill, the bay laid out below them, its fleet of small fishing boats marooned and leaning between yellow and white buoys. The light reflected brightly off the wet slate roofs and all of the houses, he noticed, had their own name signs. Trelawney. The Steep. Penmeva View. The Hoss. Penfose.

People sat on doorsteps smoking and drinking tea. Everyone smiled and bid them good morning in that light-hearted, Cornish twang.

Antony wondered if they knew about Hattie and his mum.

— Did you see the spoils as you came in?

— Sorry?

— The Little Alps, she said. Huge heaps of chalk. What's the word?

He had seen them, lit in the streetlights – they reminded him of the Hushings.

— My father, she said. Made a ton of cash from the clay pits.

— Ah. I wondered.

— What?

— The cottage and that.

— Conical, she said. Don't get me wrong, I've worked most my life. Guess.

He looked at her sideways, their footsteps clomping in time as they neared the bottom of the hill. He shrugged and she went,

— Hairdresser.

— No way.

286

— Yes way. Used to have my own salon in Lostwithiel.

— Don't tell me, you called it Choice Cuts? Hair Port?

— Try again.

— Loose Ends? Er, Sophisticut?

— Worse: Fringe Benefits. Or as your mum called it: Minge Benefits.

Their laughter echoed along the narrow, cobbled street.

He wanted to hold her.

— So what about you, she asked, how's your new job going?

— I went to the mosque this week.

— And?

— Aslaam alequm.

She squinted at him.

WITH ITS PEELING, pastel-hued weatherboard houses and higgledy-piggledy streets, the village resembled some sun-faded, woebegone postcard. The ice-cream parlours and chip shops, the rows of men fishing on the curling harbour walls, the endless soundtrack of seagulls arguing and winches grinding – it certainly had its charm. But here was a place, Antony thought, you'd want to escape.

Hattie came to an abrupt stop outside Shilley Alley and the Fountain Inn.

She seemed to be on pause.

— Did they know? Antony heard himself say.

She stared blankly across the road, body tilted forwards slightly.

— The people here, did they know about you and Mum?

It snapped her from the reverie.

— I know of six couples, she said. Lesbian couples, here in Meva.

There was laughter at the edge of her voice.

— But the place is tiny, he said.

Hattie frowned suddenly, pointing across the road.

— We discussed buying that shop.

She swallowed, eyes widening.

— Your mum and me, we were always dreaming of . . . you know.

She chewed her mouth slowly, raising her eyebrows.

— Wishing that we'd met before Lou. Before the drink.

More than anything, he wished it too, but the mention of Lou's name seemed to deplete all of his remaining energy.

— You all right, son?

— No. I'm flagging.

She took his arm.

— As your mum would say: Howay.

HE WOKE to ghosts fighting in the room, a mass of swirling colour.

She was there, stood at the foot of the bed, her back to him.

He sat up, reached out for her.

— Wait. Please.

Slowly, she began to twist.

He saw the nebulous outline of her profile.

— Mother.

He clasped his hands over his mouth as she disappeared.

The stark realization that she had died in the next room.

He ran into the corridor, calling Hattie's name.

HATTIE'S LOOK was a question he didn't know the answer to.

— 'For everything I've done in life, you've more than made up for it'.

— But she meant you?

— Yes, she said.

— What about me?

Hattie looked at her hands and nodded, displacing the tear on the tip of her nose. It fell onto the back of her hand and she rubbed it in.

— She said tell the lad I always loved him.

— You're lying.

Her eyes were full of woe.

— She was a terrible mother, he said quietly.

— You assume every woman is a natural mother, then?

He wished he'd kept his gob shut.

— Mine, she said. Hadn't a maternal bone in her body.

Hattie wiped the corners of her mouth with her serviette and pushed her plate away. She'd hardly touched the lasagne.

— So, he said. Did you not want children yourself?

As she shook her head, his eyes strayed to the photo on the fridge.

— Course I did.

— Didn't you . . . ?

— What? Do what your mum did?

Hattie placed a hand on his.

— She only lied to protect you, she said.

— But I grew up hating him. I don't want to hate him. I just don't understand how he could do what he did, what either of them did. Why'd she let Lou treat me like that?

Hattie sighed heavily. He said,

— Why'd she want me to scatter her ashes up on Swarth Coum?

— She used to go up there as a girl. She said it was this special place.

He nodded and said flatly,

— Yeah. It is.

Her anger flared again. He was finding it impossible to read her moods.

— So you're a care worker. You work with the disabled, the ill. You care for these strangers, wipe their arses, feed and bathe them, yeah?

— So?

— Alcoholism's a disease.

— Fuck that.

— Where's your compassion for Rita?

He took a deep breath.

— Growing up in that town, with lesbian parents, it wasn't like it is here. They fucking hated us.

Hattie turned away, running her fingers through her hair.

— And growing up with an alcoholic, he said. I'm sorry, but there's this anxiety you have to bear, to carry around with you. Like I was tied up in her strings. So don't tell me I'm fucking *wrong* for hating her for that. You didn't know what she was like.

Her knuckles blanched as she pulled her hair tight.

— You loosened her strings, he said. You changed her.

— Lou broke her heart so bad, your mother tried to kill herself.

Antony thinking: not for the first time.

— You didn't know that, did you? She was sectioned.

— You're aware, he said, that euthanasia's illegal?

— Oh grow up. Why, you thinking of calling the police?

The way Hattie laughed through her nose. Freely. Noisily.

— I think, he said. Think I might be a transvestite.

ANTONY PUSHED HIS CHAIR back and walked to the other side of the kitchen.

— She knew what you were getting up to, Hattie said. She thought it was just a phase. She just wanted you to be happy, but you were always so distant.

— *Me* distant?

— Rita never felt like she knew who you were.

— This is hilarious.

— She felt like she was never given the chance to know you.

— I've heard it all now.

— It was too late. We were *both* robbed of that. Do you remember when you came home in a dress and told your mum you wanted to be a girl?

She laughed gently.

— Your Aunt Val, she'd been dressing you up again. Rita thought she was losing it, that she wanted you to replace her little girl.

— Lily?

— You were a crazy fucking kid.

— Bullshit. Mum never knew me. She never let me *near* her.

— From what Rita told me, it was the other way around. You hated your own company. She said you were like that from a very young age.

Unavoidably, he knew this, and resented the fact that she knew it too.

— Lou was a bitch.

— And you were a nightmare kid from the day you were born. You were cold. You never let her near you.

— That's not . . .

— It is and you know it. You've never been happy. Ever.

He felt like he was being dismantled . . .

— Does she have a name?

And that he'd never be put back together again.

— No.

— You should give her an identity.

The anger made him want to vomit.

— You'll probably find this hard to believe, she said, but I kind of know what you're going through.

— I seriously doubt that.

— At times I feel like a man trapped inside a woman's body.

She looked herself up and down.

— I'm in drab. Dressed as a boy. I'm a tranny, too.

— You're a fucking lunatic.

— Sometimes, yes.

Hattie walked towards him, stopping at the fridge, and as they both stared at the photograph he finally knew what Hattie and his mother's love was about. It was about not judging and not being judged. It was about being friendly lovers and never having to feel alone. It was about forgetting the past and moving forward, towards brighter moments, towards a love that adjusts, transforms. Away from never absence.

Without the man.

She removed the photograph from the fridge, stared at it for a moment, and then tore it in two.

He held out his hand.

— Don't.

She dropped it in the bin.

— You've got to make sure you guard the right ones. Memories, Antony. Sometimes you remember the wrong things.

She opened the back door and walked into the garden, cupping a hand to her face.

HE THOUGHT ABOUT all the times he'd ever seen the woman, and realized she existed somewhere between states. Between sleeping and waking. Between waking and trance. Between life and last breath. Between what he knew to be real and not to be real.

Hattie was sleeping on the settee, her mouth a perfect O. He cleared his throat, coughed. No response; Hattie was fast.

He crept along the corridor to their bedroom.

On one side of the bed: the human shape of a pair of jeans, a shirt.

His mother's clothes, laid out as if she'd been lying on the bed and had simply vanished into thin air. The goldy, heart-shaped locket on her chest. The dent of her head on the pillow. Brown spots of blood.

He lifted the pillow to his face; the formless scent of his mother.

He felt strangled for words, for breath.

He dissolved into her.

THE NEXT MORNING Hattie was clearing away the breakfast dishes when she said,

— So how was it at Swarth Coum? Her ashes? Part of me wishes I could've been there, but I guessed it was something you had to do alone.

He opened his mouth, paused.

— Just give me a minute.

He left the room and went outside to his car. When he came back in he handed her the white plastic box. She looked confused.

— Part of her deserves to be down here, he said. I thought you should have half.

He touched her arm and said,

— You're the best thing that ever happened to her, you know.

— I'm sorry.

She shook her head and left the room as if she couldn't bear it.

He heard the waves coming though the open window.

THEY FOLLOWED THE STEEP Pentewan Coastal Path, up past the Coastguard Cottages and along the vertiginous cliff's edge. Panting heavily, they stopped occasionally to look out across the flat grey waters of St Austell Bay. Hattie maintained an unyielding silence, holding the box of cremains tightly to her chest.

She seemed to be avoiding his eyes.

Within an hour they reached the steps leading down Polstreath Beach. Antony was surprised by the turquoise mass of sea lushing against the slabs of cinnamon-coloured rock. The horseshoe cove, caught in a watercolour filter of soft coastal light.

He followed her down the hundred or so steps to find the beach completely deserted, and eerily free of footprints.

She took his hand as they walked towards the water's edge. The heavy sky sundered and Hattie threw him a conspiratorial smile, as if she sensed something prescient in the shock of sharp sunlight licking her skin.

She steered him towards a large rock of shimmering white granite. It looked completely out of place amid the surrounding stone. Sibilant white pebbles whooshed around its wide base.

Hattie leaned into the rock, slowly running a finger along a diametric fault line that ran through its centre, like a lightning flash.

She closed her eyes, communing with private thoughts.

THE FICKLE SEA played its kaleidoscopic hues. Along the horizon: the white isosceles of yachts and sailing boats.

She tipped the box, gently tap-tapping its sides.

They stood shoulder-to-shoulder, hand-in-hand, mutely watching the white grit and flakes float on the water's surface for a moment, before shifting, sinking.

His mother, disappearing.

Their unspoken sentiments parenthesized between the liquid sighing of the waves:

Carry her away.

XI

SPRING QUICKLY MADE its way to summer that year, and whenever he heard the static noise and felt the urge to explore the vessels in his neck, he thought about the pebbles on Polstreath Beach and felt at ease. But still he felt halted by her sporadic nightly visits, as if she revoked something in him, like his life was permanently postponed, causing a dissonant note that was neither sibilant nor silent, neither good nor bad, merely suspended.

Sometimes, the harshness of waking fully was too much and he'd open his mouth to cry out for her, thinking he'd travelled back in time and he was at home with his mother moving through the room.

He walked into the bathroom and scrutinized his reflection. Lately, he'd begun to see the soft features of his mother's face in his.

Instead of Jack's.

At Darululoom Islamia he was met with benign curiosity; at the Jamia Mosque he was met with panic and bewilderment; the surly Asian youths of Longsight and Rusholme sneered at his presence in their homes; but on the whole the selfless nature of his project elicited the amount of warmth and encouragement it deserved – especially, he found, among the mothers and sisters of the disabled.

KENNETH LOOKED around his bedroom, taking a step back.
— Kenneth?
Something flickered across his face: fear, uncertainty, fear again.
His breathing became rapid, shallow.
Antony moved towards the door, to give him some space.
— Come on, what's my name?
Wanting Kenneth to click his fingers. Wanting him to say your name is . . .
He said it again, softly,
— What's my name, Kenneth?
Kenneth looked at his feet, shrugged.

ANTONY SAT in his car outside the unit, listening to the windscreen wipers and the hollow thrum of rain on the roof. He opened the glove compartment and pulled out a slip of paper: ANTONY CUNTING DOBSON, written in Kenneth's spidery hand.

He looked back towards the unit and could see the dark shape of Kenneth at his bedroom window. Antony flashed his headlights; Kenneth pulled the curtains closed.

He drove away at speed, but soon had to pull over, his sobs filling the silences between the intermittent whirr of the windscreen wipers.

HE LEFT WORK EARLY that Friday, collected his things from the flat and began that snaking journey between the steep, broken spine of the Pennines, back to his childhood home.

HE PASSED THE SPOT where Eddie's house used to be – the house he still dreamt about. But it wasn't there any more. It had been replaced by two ugly, orange-bricked semis.

His nerves jangled.

He climbed out of the car into the town's signature odour: an uncanny fusion of vanilla and banana and chocolate coming from the ice-cream factory where his mother and Lou used to work.

He remembered the years he did the milk round, the dark early mornings, fingers numb in fingerless gloves, stealing pints off painted doorsteps to drink on the way home.

Alone on that familiar street, looking up at the sign swinging in the sweet-scented wind.

K
E
E
P
E
R
S

A
R
M
S

So there he was, in a room above a pub in the town he'd spent most of his life running away from. The room was small and dingy but they'd made a bit of an effort: kitsch draperies; a hospitality tray with a tiny kettle and some tea bags and tubs of UHT milk; a ubiquitous Jack Vettriano print hanging above the bed. There was an unrestricted view of the Market Cross and the cobbled High Street, and in the distance he could just make out the outline of Swarth Coum, fluffy white caterpillars of cloud crawling over the summit. It was as if the meaning of the world lay hidden there, as if he could read the mountain and secure some understanding from it.

His mobile vibrated. He sat down and rolled a rollie.

He would watch TV and smoke, until the window became a darkened square.

WALKING DOWN THE DIRT track, he found his eyes moving up to where the stars were making their debut.

It was still there. The dark hexagonal shape of the dovecote. The weathervane rusted towards SW. As he got to the small wooden steps, he could just make out the graffiti, door hanging off its hinges, empty plastic cider bottles, torn Rizlas packets.

And he expected to see him: Eddie, sat in the wicker chair.

He lifted his hand and rubbed the rough edge of the louvre slats, trying to remember the taut creak of wings, the doves aloft, making him blink frantically. How he asked to hold the birds in his hands, feeling their hearts beat like a really bad metaphor.

But there were no fortissimos of oo-rooing today. Just the husk of a dead bird.

He kicked the cans and cigarette packets out of the door, straightened the wicker chair, and sat down.

— EDDIE DIED this morning.

Antony was working at the high school when Ada rang. He'd gotten a job as a cleaner, blitzing the place through the summer holidays and polishing floors. It was the only work, beside the ice-cream factory, that he could find.

The news of a death, the way it focuses the mind, hardens

the senses to a distinct point of indivisibility, where nothing exists but death and decay. Getting on a bus or making a phone call or eating a sandwich or having a shower, all sensory activities experienced through the cold, hard lens of mortality.

So Antony abandoned his squeegee, and walking down the nettle-margined lane he looked up to the window Eddie used to wave from, waiting to be pushed to the pub or around the park.

The nurse hugged Antony on the doorstep.

— I'm sorry for your loss.

— What happened?

— It was very peaceful. He just squeezed my hand and was gone.

— Did he say anything?

— No. He said nowt.

The shape of Eddie in the half-light, not responding, not wishing Antony a good morning. Just the rude scratch of a clock, and cancer's saccharine stench.

He moved closer.

Eddie's eyes were like a dead rabbit's: whites yellowed, filmy. And those marks on his face: little red scratches, cuts. He'd looked so weird without the beard. Antony used to do it so well, lathering up the bowl, taking his time, Eddie's face so still as he drew the blade across.

He kissed Eddie's face, ears. He tried to close Eddie's eyes but they refused and so he kissed them too.

— I won't forget you, Eddie.

Remembering Eddie barely living, dying in that bed. Remembering the scrubby hairs on the back of Eddie's neck, the way he stroked them gently with his eyes closed, so vulnerable-looking. His scalp, paler than his face. Remembering these things because he knew that soon Eddie would be gone.

Antony took Eddie's dead body in his arms and squeezed him tight. Eddie gurgled heavily, his breath sickly in Antony's face. He dropped Eddie's body and held himself, thinking Eddie had come back to life. That he was trying to speak.

He ran from the nursing home and went up onto the moor, falling silently through himself. The same moors he'd walk at night, stood in the wilderness at the Blue Hour in a pretty dress, listening to the life in the undergrowth, feeding on the thrill of it. He slumped to a heap on the heather and dug his hands into the hard ground.

Then suddenly it was the day of the funeral, people lining the streets, tipping hats and heads as the hearse rolled by, him and Ada in the car behind, the crowd over yon park, the look on Val's face.

— I never knew he'd touched so many, Ada said.

And when Antony returned home that day, his mother told him, bold-faced,

— We want to be on our own.

Her and Lou, they wanted him out.

But then the letter and bit of money Eddie left. Antony's three lost years in black-and-white. When he got back from Poland, he stuck a pin in a map. He arrived in Manchester early one Monday and found a flat and signed on. Then he got the job at the Day Centre. It was meant to be his anti-sabbatical, a year skivvying away wiping arses to save enough to go to Australia, to get as far away as possible. But then he met Rebecca. He spent his Saturdays peering at her over the R&B section, working up the courage to ask her out. He was riddled with love.

But now he wished he'd never met her at all.

He took one last look at the dovecote, and made his way back to the pub.

THE FOLLOWING MORNING at 11:59 precisely, he was standing between the cemetery gates with a bouquet in each hand, looking up at the hands on the blue-faced church clock as they made a golden slit.

He stepped into the graveyard between the thick understorey of rhododendron, flicking Vs at the stone angels. Rounding the corner, it felt as if someone was walking at his heel, slightly out of step. He stopped and turned, heard his own breathing, and noticed the new part of the church, built after the fire all those years ago.

HE PLACED THE LILIES against the headstone and ran his fingers over the timeworn words. Eddie. The day he was born, the day he died.

Six months Ada lasted.

He recalled that terrible week after Eddie died, when Ada watched TV day and night, and the last time he saw her at the house – how she'd asked him to kill her budgie. He'd walked over to the cage; the budgie laid leaning in one corner. Ada had looked at Antony with blood-filled eyes and said,

— Wring its neck.

He'd carried the weightless bird into the backyard. It had blinked at him once, but he couldn't feel its heartbeat. He'd twisted the bird in his hands, and when he'd looked down, he had its head in one hand and the body in the other.

He looked at the daisies, the long unruly grass around the headstone. Eddie's last word: coo. The birds trapped in his head. The dark workings of it. Gone. Down into the soil. But soil can't hold that. Soil can't sing.

He pictured the three of them down in the wormy earth.

Skin. Flesh. Bone. Teeth. Nails. Hair. Blood.

How Eddie would put his knuckles to his cheek and whisper,

— Son.

The soil fat with it all.

He headed down to the bottom of the graveyard, towards fresh mounds of soil.

The interrupted earth.

HE PLACED the other bunch of flowers against Val's headstone and then read the names on the withered, faded bouquets that already rested there. One from Barry and one from Jack. But nothing from Lily. Nothing from Mikey. And he couldn't find one from his mother either.

Valerie O'Connor. Born 1947. Died 2001.

No *Beloved Mother*. No *Beloved Sister*.

Just her name and dates.

When he closed his eyes, he saw a small slab of moonlight falling through Val's curtains, revealing her unmade face: a cartoonish blur of colour. Her thumb across the cut on his eyebrow; how he'd flinched and given her a wounded look – because he wanted her to know his pain. He remembered being momentarily hypnotized by Val's touch, but he couldn't remember going home one day and telling his mother he wanted to be a girl.

There was nothing. No images. No sounds.

A void.

WALKING DOWN BRIGGATE BANK, past the pub and across the bridge to the waterfall, he noticed the westering sun had smeared the horizon an appropriately fiery pink. As a boy, he used to come here to be apart from the world, to sit beside the hubble-bubble of the beck, to smoke, to think.

The brickwork of the derelict auction rooms shot skyward to his right, broken only by windows boarded with huge sheets of graffiti'd chipboard.

He walked across the small wooden bridge and found the old, gnarled oak. Its shadow seemed to hug him.

He stood on tiptoes and peered into Cynthia's back garden.

Cynthia, his limerence. The synaesthetic mix of her deep smile, the scalpy chemical pong of the salon. Her tobacco-blonde hair and Malteser eyes.

Her body in his mind.

He looked up and recognized the branch where he used to stand, watching her windows through the halo of his parka hood.

He would dress in her underwear, holding himself.

HE CUT THROUGH the snicket and walked onto the council estate. Children in school uniforms were playing in the road. They stopped, they stared. The houses seemed so small. These streets that had held him for so long, they looked so different.

Each house held a memory. Hard scenes.

HE TURNED the corner and stopped outside his house. Children's toys lay scattered across the lawn; fancy curtains hung at the clean windows.

He looked up at his bedroom and saw himself as a boy, elbows on sill, peering up into the hills, wondering will it ever change? The nights he'd stood in the darkness of the garden, keeping warm on a wrapped bag of chips, listening to his mother and Lou inside. Looking at his old house, he wanted something to give. Mother, gone. Inside, the tears were streaming down his face, but when he put his hand up . . .

His face was dry.

He headed back to the pub, cowering through the streets of his childhood.

It was time to prepare.

IT WAS 1986. He ran back into the house and razed the tent in his bedroom, ramming things into his backpack, frantically grabbing everything he thought he might need up on Swarth Coum, and all the while, listening out for her footsteps, ready for her to return and drag him to the coal shed again. He took the bottle from beside her bed, ramming it into the bag and hurling himself down the stairs, taking firelighters, matches, bits of food from the kitchen, smashing things on the way. The pack was awkward, slapping out its burden as he mounted his bike and cycled away, snorting blood out of each nostril and fuck you is what he shouted,—FUCK YOOOOUUUU! Cracking into a scream on the *oo* sound.

PAST THE MUD-HOLE FARM, two collies shot out of their kennels, scattering a frenzy of skittish chickens. The dogs lunged at him on their hind legs, tongues lolling out, long white teeth snapping, snapping. He took a left at the top of the hill and followed the scar of footway that led to the foot of Swarth Coum. He remembered Eddie with the rifle crooked over his forearm, his chequered flat cap at a jaunty tilt. His small, pigeon-gait steps. These wild places, stained with him.

Antony gyred higher, concentrating on his step and the burn in his legs, stopping every few minutes to sit down and let the ground below him take the weight of the pack. At times it felt like his younger self was walking beside him, the adult Antony and boy Antony, walking at each other's heel.

DENUDED FIRS, canted by the winds, stood twisted like gnarled old fingers reaching for the sky. He could see the dung-coloured town a mile or so away, and the Co-op sign on the High Street was a vivid blue-and-white beacon.

He eyed the slopes on the nearby hillsides, narrow sylvan glens trailed by stanchions of electricity pylons like stroppy matchstick giants, arms akimbo. Slopes Antony used to glissade down in winter, legs in fertilizer bags, fingers burning with cold, clothes sodden with snowmelt.

Picturing his mother climbing up here as a girl, wondering what it meant for her.

He remembered the day he ran away from home, after the fight, how he'd sat on this mountain slope hugging his legs, watching the thin column of black smoke rising from the church. The box of palm leaves had exploded and the curtain and gowns went up with a *whoosh*. Sitting not far from this very spot, he'd imagined the smash of glass and pop of wood in the church below, waiting for the klaxons of fire engines to come hee-hawing through the streets, twirling their lights and causing a fair old hullabaloo.

He'd made that eye go out.

Clambering to his feet, he resumed the climb, eyeing the summit above. Beside him the wind-bent plants petered out, and soon he was above the tree line and passing between gritstone tors drenched in murky cloud.

UNDERDUSK, he reached the summit plateau. It felt like the most isolated place on Earth. The sky was ecstatic, tumultuous. Behind him, the short walk along the drovers' track to Dante's Cornice. That massive jut of escarpment, the ledge where he'd sat as a teenager, screaming into the sky, emptying the barrel-hot rifle, drinking, bagging, shuffling his arse along to the tip of the ledge. Beneath: a thousand-metre drop of sheer, razor-sharp scree. Knowing that one teensy-weensy push, one minuscule heave-ho, could send him hurtling to the rocks below. He remembered how he'd stood on that very spot and hurled the poker into the dark, and then rushed back to the tent and got Eddie's rifle. He'd lifted the barrel skyward, his mother's face: a bleary backdrop against the stars.

THE DERELICT BARN with the roof blown off. It was where it all began. Antony ran a finger along the top of the broken doorframe, caked in bird shit. The weird nostalgia of it, the way the events of 1986 were echoing his journey now, except this time he had no ropes, only fireworks and ashes.

He sat beside the pack, remembering how he'd scanned these hills one last time for some sort of clue, the clue that would get him home to Mum and Lou, to make things right. He'd slid the noose over his head and tied the running end to the top of the doorframe with a reef knot, securing it finally with a clove- and half-hitch. Taking a deep breath he'd looked out into the nothingness of Swarth Coum's high summit, he'd seen the image of his mother passed out on the kitchen floor, and so he'd pushed himself into the air, dancing in spark-light as a voice shouted down his veins, —STOP.

HE RAN for cover, worried his mother's cremains were too heavy, worried he hadn't packed them right, but he gasped as the Satellite Busters ignited, one after the other, trails of red light shooting skyward with incredible force.

Up, up, up she went.

He thought about the whispering town below, heads turning as his mother began to scream and explode in fantastic aerial bursts, staccato explosions of purple, blooming 3D globes of light, his mother bursting through the sky, flaring so brightly across the hillsides. Then a pause, followed by a fringed crimson curtain, softly falling. Charred canisters landing in back gardens.

Mother, blowing through the streets of the estate.

He walked back over to the launch site.

Embers pulsed.

Ashes danced.

XII

SOME MORNINGS he drove up over the tops, the Rover shifting through second and third past the whirring wind turbines of Coal Clough, and sometimes he parked the car and looked at the bobbled landscape of the Hushings, remembering the day he walked through there with Jade, when they sat against the humanoid boulders of Gorple Stones and moor-winds blew tears from her cheeks. And he'd think about Hattie down in Mevagissey, and felt that through her he could reconnect with a part of himself, a part that he'd forgotten.

FRANK ASKED HIM to take a seat. Shaking his head, he opened the final draft of Antony's report and began to read,

— Implementation of Interim Measures. Methodology and Research Techniques. Local Topography. Summary of Interview Responses and Focus Group Meetings. Current Service Provision and Mapping Exercise. Options for Integrated Community Provision. I mean?

Frank flicked the front of the report and laughed good-humouredly.

— Is it not detailed enough? Antony asked.

— Have you any idea how *good* this is? Honestly, Ant . . .

— Thanks.

— Head Office, they've had everyone on the phone: the

Asian Disability Network; Multicultural Liaison officers; the imams you've visited. All of them singing your praises.

— That's great, really. I'm honoured. But what happens now? I don't think I can go back to cleaning arses. Don't send me back to the dark place, Frank.

— Well, you've still got a few weeks to get this distributed yet.

— And translated into Urdu.

— Don't worry, Frank said. I'll see what I can do.

THE NET BECAME something of a saviour. There was a whole world out there at the click of a mouse, a whole community who knew something of what he was going through, and he felt as if he'd stepped through the back of the wardrobe. Chat rooms and support networks and fetish sites, interminable information on make-up and clothes and wigs and femme forms, TVs surfing the Net in their virtual closets, millions of them speeding down the superhighway in their six-inch heels.

He found the names and addresses of all the tranny-friendly bars around Canal Street, and most had dressing rooms, so you didn't have to worry about being stabbed to death en route.

He'd even found a tranny clothes shop.

He straightened the orange and brown chequered rug over the upside-down question mark, and then repositioned the painting on the mantelpiece. It wasn't the best painting he'd ever done, but it was his first effort in years, and the nostalgic smell of the linseed and turpentine made him swoon. Next to the painting sat the photograph of him and Daniel that Carla had taken at the airport.

Daniel's smile in the picture: an invitation.

He stood before the window, the city sky cadmium-orange in the closing day.

She'd be here soon.

On the window was a square Post-it note. He read it aloud,
— Finestra.

Along with the new rugs and brightly coloured throws and the colourful large canvas, Catalan nouns decorated his flat on yellow Post-it notes:

CORBERTS
PLAT i BOL
LAVABO
CAMBRA
ESCRIPTORI

He wondered whether Carla was pregnant yet.

The smell of baking pizza and bubble bath filled the flat.

He pulled a long pink hair from his dressing gown and held it up to the light. Persian Rose. He pulled it through his lips, over his tongue, and let it fall to the carpet.

He remembered meeting Jade in the Fox and Goose, and how he thought he'd never see her again. And she was right: there was only room for one woman in his life right now.

He watched the city wink outside.

He didn't have to wait very long.

SPARKLE HAPPINESS
SUNSHINE GRINNING
POWERFUL LOVING
GLITTERING EXCITING
RICHNESS RADIANT
CHEEKY BLISS LAUGHTER
HILARIOUS JOYFUL
EXUBERANT SENSUOUS
VIBRANT BEAUTIFUL
HARMONY YOU!

THEY STOOD LOOKING at the outfit laid across the bed.

The excitement of doing it in public, of presenting himself to the outside world. The clothes were like something explosive in the room – volatile, vying for attention. They couldn't keep their eyes off the dress, the tights, the heels.

The consummation of his fantasy.

I'll look awful, he thought. I'll look totally shit.

And he knew what Hattie was thinking – it reminded her of his mother's clothes, spread out across her bed.

Hattie said wow again.

— I'm scared, he said. I'm fucking bricking it.

Hattie let the fabric of the dress run between her fingers.

— You're going to be amazing.

His fantasy incarnated.

— You going to put this lot on, then?

Suddenly he didn't want to do this, to be like this, to have this drive.

Heat prickled his cheeks. He coughed into his fist for no reason.

— Did she really say I was a bad son?

Hattie turned him by the shoulders.

— I should never have said that. I was upset.

— It was like half of my life was always missing, he said.

— Jack?

328

— I loved a man I'd never met. It's stupid.

— No, Ant. It's not. It just makes you human.

He felt Hattie's smile on the inside.

— I may be some time, he said.

— There's no rush.

— There's pizza on the kitchen table. The remote's over there. There's a bottle of wine in the fridge. Whatever. Shit.

— You've waited all of your life for this, son.

He picked up his dress, tights, heels.

He took the new wig from its stand.

— Fuck it, he said. Let's do it.

THANKS

Thank you Olivia Woolley for your counsel, friendship and inspiration. Thank you Pia, Dr Richard Curtis, Nikki, DeDe, Caroline Greene, and Vicky Lee at the WayOut club for advice on all things tranny. Thank you Sara Maitland for your generous editorial support. Thank you Dr Anna-lyse Rowe for your analytical laser beam. Thank you Clare Allan, Chris Crouch, Laura West, Delia Jarrett-Macauley, Julia Bird and especially Andy Ching for being such thoughtful readers. Thank you Dr Chris Evans for your support. Thank you Annie Clarkson for driving me around Manchester and listening to the gripes. Thank you *Transmission* and *Succour* magazines where extracts of this novel first appeared. Thank you Sam Humphreys for your patience and persistence. Thank you Dana Captainino for helping me secure the grant. Thank you Ralph Wilde for taking me to the WayOut club for the first time dressed as a gay cowboy. Thank you Liam Relph for your outstanding design skills. Thank you Ledig House, New York, where I completed this novel. Thank you Lynne for far too many things to list. And for the generosity of Arts Council England – whose grant enabled me to write full-time while working on this novel – I am deeply grateful.